At Home

a selection of stories by

Franz Hohler

D1595688

books

At Home
a selection of stories by Franz Hohler

The stories in this collection have been translated from the German by various translators. For the titles of the original texts in German, publishers, translators, credits and permissions see page 169.

Copyright © 2009 Bergli Books

Published with the support of
Pro Helvetia, Swiss Arts Council
Lotteriefonds Kanton Solothurn

Cover photograph © Christian Altorfer,
Zurich, www.altocard.ch

Bergli Books   Tel.: +41 61 373 27 77
Rümelinsplatz 19   Fax: +41 61 373 27 78
CH-4001 Basel   e-mail: info@bergli.ch
Switzerland   www.bergli.ch

ISBN 978-3-905252-18-7

Table of Contents

At Home

I'm at home when my hand reaches out at just the right height for the light switch.

I'm at home when my feet automatically know the exact number of steps on the stairs.

I'm at home when I get annoyed with the neighbour's dog who barks when I go out into my garden.

If the dog didn't bark, something would be missing.

If my feet didn't know the stairs, I'd fall.

If my hand wouldn't find the light switch, it would be dark. ooo

My Mother's Father

His parents died when he was a child and he spent his youth as a poorly treated Verdingbub* as described in the stories by Jeremias Gotthelf. But he managed to complete his studies at a technical school and became a telephone technician. He married a woman who had also grown up as an orphan. They brought four children into the world, and as everything had turned out so well, my grandfather apparently remembered his secret creed. This creed that stayed with him through the hard times of his life must have been something like a belief in beauty, because at 41, my grandfather decided to learn to play the cello.

How did he do that? Did he borrow a cello? Did he go to a cello teacher? No, he went to a violin maker and ordered a cello from him. Only when he had the instrument — and it could not have been cheap since Mr. Meinel in Liestal was a well-known violin maker — did he look for a cello teacher who told him, however, after the second or

---

*Verdingbub: Between about 1800 and 1950 the authorities in some Swiss communities could hold public auctions for the care of orphans. The family accepting the least for room and board could have the orphan mostly for forced labour on farms and usually with no pay. Still loved Swiss writer Jeremias Gotthelf (pseudonym for Albert Bitzius, 1797 - 1854, a clergyman) wrote about Verdingkinder in his novel *Bauernspiegel* showing the misery of the poor and the deplorable state of orphans in such a situation.

third lesson, that there was no point in continuing since his fingers were too small for the fingering needed to play the cello.

At this point in the story my grandfather used to show me his left hand and stick out his little finger to prove it wasn't big enough to play the cello properly.

So he put the instrument aside and joined a mandolin club. It was surely more fun than cello lessons and the fingering was easier. For years he had to make payments for the cello. Only recently I found the bundle of receipts in a family drawer showing the monthly installments. He arranged for his daughters to have private violin and piano lessons — my mother was a good violinist her whole life — but his son wasn't interested in the cello.

And then the next generation arrived.

My older brother also learned to play the violin and when my parents asked me when I was 10 years old which instrument I wanted to play — we had a piano and a cello at home — I said without hesitation: the cello. I started with a 3/4 instrument, but soon my hands and my little finger were big enough that I could play my grandfather's cello and this is the cello I still play today. And when I sing my chansons, I accompany myself on it.

Without my grandfather's persevering belief in beauty, his instrument would not have waited for me. And maybe it was only I, two generations later, who was able to fulfil his creed — also I am persevering enough to stick to *my* creed: What you feel is good for you, you simply have to do! ∞

The Tragic Centipede

The old centipede was sitting in front of his cave and finally wanted to count his feet. He had wanted to do that his whole life but there was always something preventing him from doing so. Now, at last, he had a little bit of time and started counting his feet.

But the life of a centipede is very hard. Just as he reached his 218th foot he had to jump into the cave to save himself from being eaten by a crested tit. That would not have been necessary because, as everybody knows, crested tits are vegetarians. So the old centipede grumpily had to start counting all over again. He got to his 432nd foot when his 810th started itching so badly that he scratched himself with the following dozen, and that got him so confused that he lost count and had to start all over again. This time he got to the 511th, when his wife showed up with the shoemaker's bill. Furiously he threw the paper on the floor, trampled it with his feet and sat down in front of his cave determined not to let himself be interrupted by anything else. He was only at his 203rd foot when the crested tit ate him (by mistake — that is the tragedy) and so he never learned just how many feet he really had.

Let us pray. ∘∘∘

Alternatours (a one-man act on stage)

Oh, I almost forgot to ask you something: Have you already filled out the questionnaire? The one included in the last monthly bulletin about 'Alternatours'? It's on the book table. You can still do it. Or haven't you heard about 'Alternatours'? They're from the charity travel office that arranges holidays that are well, let's say, different.

Well, it's like this. When we go someplace on vacation, then we always expect to see some natives for us to photograph. That already starts before we leave our own country. When we go to a mountain village in summer, somebody has to be out there working to bring in the hay, and we also want to see a few cows. And the guy tending the sheep might be an Albanian, but he has to be wearing a local cheese-maker's cap.

And when we go to a Portuguese fishing village, then we expect the fisherman to be working, and to return from the sea in the morning with a tough look on his face and a boat full of fish. Without that, you can forget having a party to show slides of your vacation. And we'd be really surprised if we went to Guatemala and all the natives with the colorful scarves were away on vacation, for example, in Switzerland.

When you go on vacation you need to have a certain amount of alienation. Genuine natives don't really need to go on vacation at all. Or how do you explain the fact that while you're strolling over the Lägern mountain you're unlikely to meet up with a group of Portuguese fishermen coming your way who are spending their hiking vacation in Switzerland?

Or has it ever happened to you that while you are having a barbecue in your garden, a few Senegalese shepherds take photographs of you over the garden fence so that they have something to show about Swiss traditions when they get home?

Or that when you're shopping at Oerlikon market, an Indian woman takes a picture of you because she wants to bring back to the Altiplano a picture of all the colours at our organic fruits and vegetable stand in front of the Hotel International?

You see, that's how Alternatours helps people from the Third World get an impression of the First World. They don't only make such a trip possible, but it's combined with a photography course. And for that they're looking for people here who'll let themselves be photographed doing everyday activities, and the questionnaire is so that you can give your agreement to being photographed.

Now, what do we have to fill out?

Under 'occupation', that's where you have to watch what you write. If you put 'farmer', it's possible that a dark-skinned tourist will drop by sometime and take a photo of you on your tractor or on your hay tedder or on the manure spreader, like we do when we take photos in

Paraguay of the farmers on their ox-drawn carts. Or if you put that you are a 'central-heating technician', the tourist will show up at the construction site wanting to take a picture of a typical Swiss day just as you're down in a pithole sealing off a pipe.

Whether you live in the city or in the country is, of course, very important. You put that where it says 'place of residence' as that can possibly give quite different pictures.

Let's say you're in a town. Your guest can go with you to a tram stop and take a picture of you putting a coin in the ticket dispenser, and of the look on your face when you realize that you've got ten centimes too little, and how you go to a kiosk to buy a BLICK newspaper just so you get a two-franc coin back as change to put in the ticket machine to be able to get to the train station. And he can take a photo of you trying to disentangle a luggage cart from a long row of them stuck together. He can get some terrific photos that way. Or maybe he can take a picture of you putting part of your rubbish in a public waste container so that you can save on the fee for garbage bags, or some other typical picture of life in a Swiss town.

You're asked to write down your kind of 'festivities planned'. You can put there that you'll soon go to a christening or a wedding. Or if there's going to be a funeral soon, that's always something really interesting. We always take pictures of that too when we go to a foreign country and there's a whole procession of mourners all on one truck riding together with the coffin. Those are very impressive photos. So our dark-skinned guest should also be able to join the funeral ceremonies and take pictures at the burial sites too. You have to take all those questions into consideration.

You're asked to answer questions about your family, about your pets and your preferences for music. You know how important music is in developing countries — just think of the rhythms of African drums or of the Balinese temple dances, or the flutes of the Andes. Would you let someone take a photo of you putting a Tina Turner CD in your CD disk player? Or of your son playing a little local music? And your guest could go along with him to the air-raid shelter in your neighborhood and take a flash shot of him with his friends playing 'Enter Sandman' by the Metallica band?

And where the form asks you to mention your 'rituals', that's of course also interesting. There you can write in 'mowing the lawn', 'washing the car', 'playing cards on Saturdays', 'bowling' or 'Sunday mountain hiking'. (It's a good idea to write there 'Attention, red socks' so that your guest is sure on that day to take along a color film.)

Or there is also an interesting question: 'Do you frequently wait in lines?' That refers of course to the fact that in Third World countries there's a lot of waiting for certain things. Therefore our guest would surely be interested in finding out where the waiting lines are here. Can he wait in line with you at the end of the month and take a picture of you at the post office while you're paying your bills, or of you in front of an ATM cash dispenser on a Saturday?

The questionnaire asks a lot more questions, what kind of dances you do, sports, shopping habits, children, travels, employees, household help, etc., etc. — if you're interested, as I said, you can go get a questionnaire at the book table and take it with you so that you can think about whether you want to make yourself available as an ethno model. That'd be great. But you'd have to accept the fact that sooner or later at a slide show at adult evening classes in Cameroon, slides will be shown of you stuck in a traffic jam waiting to get through the Gotthard tunnel with a surfboard on your roof, and the lecture will be titled something like 'Switzerland, the Last Nomads of the Alps'. ₀₀₀

Conditions for Taking Nourishment

I know the case of a child who didn't want to eat anything anymore once it was one year old. When you wanted to give him his mashed-up baby food, he'd throw his hands in front of his face, shake his head and turn around so that it was impossible to get even one spoonful in his mouth. If you succeeded in finally putting a bite in his mouth, he'd spit it all out and start screaming. The only thing he'd allow in his mouth was a bit of water. But when you gave him some milk instead, he'd want nothing of it.

His parents were worried and could not understand what caused this sudden change. They first tried to convince the child to eat his baby food by pleading, then by threatening and even by smacking him. It was all useless. They put a banana in front of him, something he had always eaten before, but the child wouldn't take it. The solution to the problem was found by accident. The child's room was closed off by a gate mounted in the door frame so that the child could be left in the room with an open door and the parents could hear what was going on inside without the child being able to run out of the room.

On the third day of the child's refusal of any nourishment, the father wanted to hand in the baby food to the mother who was already in the room to put the child to bed.

The child ran to the gate and looked up longingly at the plate. Right away, the father bent down over the gate and started to spoon in the baby food. And the child, who was gripping the bars of the gate with both hands and whose head came to just over the top of the gate, seemed to be very pleased and ate everything.

The next morning the father fed the child in the same way before he went to work and the child didn't show the slightest resistance. But when the mother wanted to feed the baby over the gate at lunch, he ran away and kept opening and closing the lid of his toy chest with loud bangs until the mother moved away from the gate. In the evening he accepted the food from the father over the gate without a fuss.

Now the child was eating again, but the fact that he only wanted his father to feed him created a problem for the parents. Besides the fact that the child now only got two meals a day, it was not easy for the father to be home on time every evening to feed his child since his job often required him to be out of town. Once he came a little late and heard the child already screaming. He quickly threw his coat over a chair, rushed to the child's room and fed him over the gate. Only afterwards did he realize that he had forgotten to take off his hat. When he went to feed the child the next morning, the child pointed incessantly at his father's head and refused to eat. Then the father remembered the previous evening, fetched his hat and put it on. Happily the child let himself be fed the baby food. From now on the father always had to have his hat on if he wanted the child to eat.

So far the mother had always been present when the child received his food. But once when she had not slept well, she stayed in bed longer since the father had offered to take care of the child alone. However, the child refused to eat the baby food without the mother being present. This left the father no choice. He had to fetch the mother who sat down in her nightgown on a child's chair.

That same evening the child resisted, screaming at the impertinence of having to eat the baby food even though everything was in order. The father stood outside the gate with his hat on and the mother was also present. Admittedly she was wearing her normal clothes, and since the child kept pointing at her again and again, in the end she put on her nightgown and returned to the room. The child was, however, only satisfied when she sat on the little children's chair and watched the child eating.

From then on, the mother always had to put on her nightgown at mealtimes, otherwise there was no chance of the child eating his food.

Soon the child was no longer influenced by coincidental things happening that he wanted repeated, but he began to think up new requirements on his own. Once he pointed to the wardrobe in the room and looked at his mother. The mother went to the wardrobe and was going to open it but the child screamed and pointed to the top of the closet. The mother said no, she would not do that. The child lay down on the floor kicking about with his hands and feet and letting out the most disagreeable, ear-piercing screams. In spite of this, the parents decided they could not go along with this wish of the child, and so he had to go to bed without eating anything, just until the next morning when they hoped he would surely have forgotten the idea.

The next morning when the mother was sitting in her nightgown on the child's chair and the father stood in front of the gate with his hat on and they were set to feed the child, he again refused to eat and pointed to the top of the wardrobe closet. The parents did not give in to this wish, and the child ate nothing.

Two days later, as he was showing signs of weakness since he had not had anything but water, the parents gave in. In her nightgown the mother climbed to the top of the wardrobe and stretched out flat. Immediately the child started eating his baby food with great enthusiasm while keeping his eyes on the mother to be sure she was really watching him eating. After suffering this defeat, the parents became very worried about what would happen in the future. It is debatable whether their behaviour was right or not, but they could think of nothing else to do to keep the child from starving to death. The paediatrician, who always decided in favour of the child and against the parents, advised them urgently to give in to the wishes of the child since it was more important that the child ate than that the parents had an easy time. And a child psychologist the father knew was also unable to help and spoke of a premature manifestation of the terrible twos and gave them vague hopes that this condition was of a temporary nature only.

But there was no sign of this. The next time the child was supposed to eat, he ran to the window and could not be taken away from it. The father brought the child's attention to the mother, who was correctly lying on top of the closet in her nightgown, and to the hat on his head, and tried to feed the child over the gate. But the child shook his whole body and held on to the windowsill with both hands. The father didn't even want to consider it but knew what that meant. The room was upstairs, so he got a ladder from the cellar and propped it up against the house from outside, climbed up to the child's room and fed the child his baby food through the open window. The child was delighted and ate everything.

The next day it was raining and the father climbed the ladder to the child's room with an umbrella. From then on he always had to come to the window with the umbrella regardless of the weather. Otherwise the baby food was not eaten.

In the meantime the parents had hired a maid to help them out. The child rejected her completely and only wanted to be taken care of by the mother. Also their hope that the maid could lie on top of the wardrobe in the mother's nightgown was shattered. The child almost had a fit of raving madness at this clumsy attempt of deception. But as the maid was going to leave the room, things did not get better. She had to stay at the gate and also watch as the child was eating. But not only that, he only ate if the maid shook a rattle whenever he swallowed a spoonful of food.

One would assume that was about as bad as things could get, but then the child started pushing the father away when he leaned over the windowsill. And he now pitched the bowl with the baby food that the father put on the windowsill out the window. The father had no choice but to purchase an extremely high, stabilized double ladder. He positioned it at a small distance from the wall of the house, climbed to the top and gave the baby food to the child with a spoon attached to a bamboo pole. In order to dip this spoon in the baby food, he had to hold the bowl in his left hand with his arm stretched out, as it was impossible now to set the bowl with the baby food on the ladder. Since he could not appear without the umbrella and could not hold it in his hand, he constructed a device out of wire that could be mounted on his shoulders and to which he attached the umbrella so that it would be at about the same height as if he had held it in his hand.

A neighbour looking at the house just then through binoculars sees the following:

The father is standing on a stabilized double ladder outside the window of the first floor and reaches out with a spoonful of baby food that has been attached to a bamboo pole. He is wearing a hat and an umbrella in a wire construction fixed to his shoulders. The mother is lying on top of the wardrobe and the maid is standing in front of the gate mounted in the doorframe. Both the mother and the maid are watching as the child eats and the maid, in addition, just as each spoon of baby food is swallowed, shakes a rattle.

Only when all these conditions have been met, and only then, will the child eat. ∘∘∘

The Monkey and the Crocodile

A monkey was bitten by a crocodile and went to his friend, the hippopotamus, and told him what had happened. The hippopotamus thought about it for a long time, then went to an elephant to tell him what had happened. The elephant thought about it a long time, ate 80 kilos of bananas and then went to tell the lion what had happened. The lion knew immediately what to do. He fetched a swarm of hornets and sent them to the crocodile. But the hornets didn't know which crocodile they should bite. Word about them got to the crocodile and he went to his friend, the condor. He fetched a swarm of wasps and sent them to fight against the hornets. The swarms flew against each other and there was a tremendous air battle while the monkey, the crocodile, the hippopotamus, the elephant, the lion and the condor watched from below, and each of them cheered for their team. When the hornets and the wasps saw that the monkey, the crocodile, the hippopotamus, the elephant, the lion and the condor were only watching them, they decided to make peace with each other and went straight to attack the condor, the lion, the elephant, the hippopotamus, the crocodile and the monkey. They all returned home stung and talked about this battle for a long time. ₒₒₒ

The Pet

I have a pet.

One day, because I am alone so much, I felt the need to have something living around me, a creature that would follow me with its eyes when I went away in the morning and would jump up and down when I returned home in the evening. Since this feeling lasted for several days, I decided to yield to it and went to a pet shop.

Right from the beginning my eyes fell on something furry, but it wasn't easy to find an animal that suited my indefinite yet quite precise ideas. The trouble was that I couldn't say what I really wanted. I only knew that I didn't want the animals that were on view. A hamster, for example, would have been interesting, but I feared that it would hardly take any notice of me; guinea pigs and white mice also didn't appeal to me for the same reason, and the latter also turned me off because I saw no sense in their frantic activity. A dog, on the other hand, would have demanded too much of me, while I would have resented it every time a cat stayed away from home. The pigmy rabbits on sale in the pet shop seemed at first to be something like what I was looking for, but then suddenly I was disturbed by their having been demeaned through overbreeding, behind which I also suspected a dwarfing of their emotional life. A monkey seemed to me so full of compulsive activity that I could not bear to keep it in a cage. And that exhausted the selection of furry animals.

I asked the shopkeeper again, and then, from the room behind the shop, he brought out a cage in which a little furry clump lay in a corner beside a feeding basin. I knew immediately that I wanted this animal. The shopkeeper told me it had just arrived from Malaya and, since its papers had been lost in transit, he didn't even know what the creature was. It was probably something like a sloth or an opossum. The animal had not yet unrolled itself, he said, and he would like to keep it in the shop a bit longer.

But I offered him so high a price that he immediately agreed to the sale. He gave me a few suggestions about feeding along the lines of what one would give a monkey: fruit, peanuts, fresh water every day, and a mixture of vitamin-enriched grain, of which I bought a sack. I also bought an orris root for the animal's teeth, and then I left the shop and carried the cage, which was fairly large, back to my place where I put it on a bureau.

I sat down in front of the cage and waited an hour or two, but the clump of fur didn't move. I couldn't even see if it was breathing. But when I poked a finger through the bars and touched its fur, it was warm. I put half of a peeled banana in the cage, a cut-up apple and some vitamin-enriched grain, filled the little basin with fresh water and left the apartment. When I came back late in the evening and turned on the light, I saw that the food was still just as I had left it, but the water had been drained dry.

The next morning the animal still lay in the corner of its cage and had eaten nothing. The banana and apple had turned brown, so I took them out, replaced them with fresh ones and filled the water bowl again. In the evening, when I returned, the food was untouched but the bowl was empty and now one paw poked out from beneath the fur. Actually the paw was more like a hand. It had five black, wrinkled, slightly hairy fingers which, as near as I could see, had extraordinarily sharp nails. Some kind of monkey after all, I thought. Then I touched the hand with the tip of my finger and it was immediately withdrawn beneath the fur once more.

The creature seemed to need no food at all. It merely drained its water bowl twice a day, and it was a long time before I saw more than isolated parts of it. The next thing after the little hand was a tail that I suddenly found hanging out of the cage, and the length of which surprised me. When I touched it, it seemed slack and unmuscular, and it seemed inconceivable that the animal could use it to cling to a branch. I was also amazed at the tuft at the end of the tail. But as soon as I pulled on it the tail disappeared again beneath the clump of fur.

I now assumed that the creature was either a sloth or some kind of meerkat, until one morning I saw a foot. It was peeking out from under the fur, and there was no doubt about it, the foot was a hoof and the hoof was split in the middle. I checked the encyclopedia and found that this condition was native to the so-called artiodactyls — that is, my pet must belong to the same family as camels, deer or giraffes. The only thing I could imagine was that it might possibly be a very tiny dwarf goat, but then the hand that I had seen so clearly was incomprehensible. The encyclopedia also said: "Many extinct species." Perhaps, I thought, perhaps I've stumbled on an animal that's really extinct. The thought pleased me and I now also had an explanation for the fact that the animal seemed to live without eating, since the encyclopedia related that cloven-hoofed animals chew their cud. Apparently this was an extinct species of cloven-hoofed creature with a remark-ably long cud-chewing time.

These assumptions were all false. I learned the species to which my pet belonged one Sunday morning when I had my radio on. Some festive music for strings had just ended and the announcer introduced the broadcast of a Catholic mass. This was followed by a rasping shriek from the cage. I turned around and saw that my pet had humped up and was gripping the bars of the cage with both hands. Now I realized that it was a devil.

I immediately turned the radio off and spoke soothingly to the animal. I noticed that every hair on its body was standing up straight and that it trembled in every limb. Its eyes looked fearfully in the direction from which the voice had come, and it seemed to me that its glance held not only fear but also hatred. At the same time, I noticed that the beast had two tiny horns on its forehead. It was a proper devil all right.

During the rest of the day, while the creature slowly calmed down and stared out of its cage, its head leaning against the orris root, I considered what I ought to do. I could think of nothing, no particular steps to take, and I didn't really want to do anything, I had nothing against keeping a devil as a pet and I intended to go right on living as I had before.

The changes came gradually. The first thing I noticed was that the devil, when he wasn't lying there rolled up in a ball, could find no comfortable position. His body seemed made for an upright posture and there was something unnatural about him lying there like a dog, yet he did not seem to be able to sit up properly and fold his hands around his knees. I built him a little chair on which he took to frequently sitting in a rather ladylike fashion, both legs on the same side.

Still he didn't seem quite satisfied and so I hit on the idea of making him a hammock, which I fastened between the bars of the cage. He was enthusiastic about it, often lying in it the entire day and swinging back and forth. Soon he had the inspiration of letting his tail dangle down into the water basin so that, when he was thirsty, he dipped its tuft in the water, brought it up again and licked it.

Up to this point he had taken nothing but water, but now he began, whenever I ate, to look at me in a way that I found unpleasant. He would jump from his hammock, pull himself upright against the bars of the cage and hang on with his hands, staring incessantly at my plate. I felt his glance at my back and at first, since I was annoyed, I tried to eat so that I was facing him. But now I found his glance even more unbearable. Then you eat too, I said to him, and held out a noodle. He merely turned his head away briefly and then looked at me again. I cut him a piece of my cutlet and offered it to him. He grabbed it and stuffed it into his mouth. He chewed it very quickly and gulped it down. I gave him another piece, which he treated in the same fashion. Finally, I opened the little door of the cage and put in the remaining bone, and to my surprise he did not gnaw at it but quickly ate the entire thing. When he saw that I was finished eating, he returned to his hammock and rocked back and forth.

Now that I knew that the devil ate too, I offered him all possible foods, but he wanted only meat. He wouldn't even accept fish, and when I tried to give him something cheap, tripe or a chicken heart, he merely turned his head to the side, and sometimes he hissed. It had to be good meat, the same as I ate myself, and he wouldn't take it raw, only cooked. Soon he became so insistent that I had to give him an entire piece each time; I began shopping for two, and the butcher smiled when he cut the meat for me.

Now I must mention something that is not very appetizing but which became very important for me. As long as the devil had been content with only water, I had never seen any excrement, not even urine; his body had apparently absorbed every last drop. But with his eating, he began defecating in little piles that were almost liquid, like someone with diarrhea. When he squeezed out his turd, some of it always ran down his legs, where it would dry and become crusty. The excrement had a repellent odor, so that every evening I had to clean the entire cage and wipe the devil's legs with an alcohol-soaked rag. What especially disgusted me was that he always dumped his load in the water basin, which I was therefore compelled to clean thoroughly each time. Often he pissed between the bars of the cage with obvious pleasure, which forced me to cover in plastic the top of the bureau on which the cage stood.

All of this meant a lot of work, besides which the stink gradually began to sink in so that it didn't quite disappear even after the daily cleaning. I considered hanging the cage in front of the window, but I had noticed that the devil's teeth began to chatter if I even aired the room for a quarter of an hour. He obviously preferred the warmth.

After I had cleaned his legs, a process which he permitted with pleasure, I let him run around in the apartment a bit. He did not move very gracefully, walking upright on his two legs, and when he wanted to look at something high up I had to lift him, an operation which he usually requested with an upward gesture of the head and a brief cough. The first time I lifted him in front of my bookcase where he wanted to look at the top shelf, he immediately grabbed a book, threw it to the floor, jumped down and trampled on it with angry howls until it was in tatters. It was the Bible.

His aversion to everything linked with religion became more evident from day to day. One time he wanted to look at a landscape that hung in the hallway, and after I had lifted him up, he broke the glass of the frame with a sharp lunge of his hoof, and with his claws he ripped out a church steeple that was painted so far back on the horizon that I had never before noticed it.

He was most difficult on Sundays. Everytime the church bells called people to church, the devil began to whimper, crouched in one corner of the cage, and looked at me so sadly and despairingly that I was forced to try and deal with his pain. At first I didn't know what to do. I closed the shutters and the window and pulled the curtains so that the bells sounded muffled, but the devil continued to look just as miserable. I showed him the veal intended for his lunch, but he looked almost insulted. I began to sing so loudly that you couldn't hear the bells any more, but it was no use. At this point I usually gave up all effort, but by now it was impossible for me to concentrate on anything else. Once I became so furious that I threw the shutters open with a curse and left the window ajar as well. The devil immediately became quiet and looked at me with a grateful glance. The rest of that Sunday was undisturbed, and when toward evening the bells began to torture him again I swore loudly again and he calmed down.

But he became increasingly demanding, and soon I could console him only by holding his hand while the bells rang and swearing softly but insistently. If once I neglected to do this, he became tearful again. And if I walked away from the cage, he broke out in sobs that racked his whole body. Although I am not religious, after a while the constant cursing on Sundays began to affect me. Nevertheless, I have still not brought myself to leave the devil alone on a Sunday because the thought of him spending the entire day howling and miserable in his cage makes me feel inhuman.

But that is not my biggest problem. What concerns me most right now is the question of how I am to get the stench out of the apartment. Having failed with the usual room sprays, I have become a customer of homeopathic and health food shops.

Now, for example, my rooms are festooned with little sacks of organically grown, dried jasmine blossoms which I moisten each day with an anthroposophical lavender oil. But I have observed to my horror that the devil's smell has lately begun clinging to my own person, though I only notice it at special moments, such as when I sweat from the armpits.

I can see that it will not be long before I smell like my devil. It is not a country odor, barn-like; if it were, I could move to a farm in order to justify it. No, it is an almost indescribable mixture of something biting, like burning rubbish; something foul, like the water in a vase of flowers which has stood for too long; and something breathtaking, like decaying corpses. Anyone who smells like that cannot go out among people, would not dare to go into a shop, restaurant, post office, not to mention his job.

If you have followed me this far, you will doubtless advise me — and by all the rules of reason it would be correct — to get rid of this pet as quickly as possible. But that is just what I cannot do. I have grown attached to the devil; I am touched by his look when he wants something; I have the feeling he needs me and would suffer a lamentable end if I did not devote all my energies to his care. Besides, how could I do it? I couldn't bring myself to go back to the pet shop. It would be impossible for me to toss him into the water in a sack, and he seems too little like an animal for me to bring him to a veterinarian for a shot; besides, I don't know what a vet would say if I turned up with a devil during consulting hours.

I didn't dare confide in anyone. For a while I considered consulting a minister, but first I looked through some theological literature and observed that these days, even in conservative circles, people are well past believing in the existence of an actual physical devil; instead they somehow conceive of evil as something spiritual. I do not want to blur this praiseworthy concept with my own case.

And there is something else. I have the feeling that the destruction of the devil would have grave consequences for me. I can neither explain this feeling nor make it more precise. I simply believe that something sinister would happen to me and I am afraid. I would rather keep my devil and go on living with him in the same manner as before.

What else can I do? ₀₀₀

The Goddess

In the beginning, before the world was created, God was wandering around through the nothingness trying to find something. He had almost given up hope and was dead tired when suddenly he came to a big shed. He knocked. A goddess opened the door and asked him to come in.

She said she was just busy working on Creation but he should take a seat for a while and watch what she was doing. At the moment she was planting various water plants in an aquarium.

God was astonished at what he saw. He would never have come up with the idea of creating a substance like water. It is precisely this, the Goddess said smilingly, that was, so to speak, the basis of life.

After a while God asked if perhaps he could help a bit and the Goddess said she would be very grateful if he could take the water and the things she had created so far to one of the planets that she had set up a little further in the back. She would like to start with the least significant one as a test.

So God began to deliver the Goddess' creations one after the other from her shed to the earth, and it is not a surprise that later, people on this planet knew only about

Franz Hohler

the God who had brought it all and who they assumed was the actual creator of it all.

Of the Goddess who had thought it all up, however, they knew nothing, and therefore it's high time she gets mentioned. ∘∘∘

35

The Deception

Rusterholz is a good name for a man who had experienced what I am about to tell you. Charles Rusterholz was approaching forty and worked for a travel firm.

He had just saved someone's life when he entered the small shop at the railway station which was open extended hours. He had been standing at a red light on a traffic island at the pedestrian crossing. On the two-lane street the traffic lights for the first lane were red, but they were green for the second lane. Two or three cars were waiting in the first lane. Then a boy with a skateboard pushed past him to cross the street. "Watch out!" shouted Rusterholz, seeing a car approaching in the second lane. The boy braked and the car brushed past him. The boy turned round startled, and Rusterholz told him he should watch out when the lights were red. A woman standing next to him had said and done nothing but just held her hand to her mouth. The man opposite, who had had a better view of the approaching car than he did, had not done anything either to prevent the accident. In retrospect, Rusterholz suspected both of them of wanting to watch how an accident happened.

Continuing on his way, he wondered why he hadn't made a greater appeal to the boy's conscience by warning him that it could have cost him his life. He also realised that both he and the woman had crossed the first section of road as far as the island on red, because it was for trams only, and it was obvious that there weren't any coming. The youngster with the skateboard must then have followed their example, and for that Rusterholz was partly to blame. He also thought of his own ten-year-old son. He certainly intended to tell him this story. He decided that from now on, he would always stop at pedestrian crossings when the light was red, even if there were no vehicles in sight. On the whole, he was pleased that he had reacted at all because he was not really used to exercising authority. He avoided situations that called for any sort of intervention, always giving the widest possible berth to drunks on the bus or to punks with tattered rucksacks, and to dogs with a red bandana instead of a leash.

These thoughts were still going through his mind as he was paying at the cash register for the three litres of milk his wife had asked him to get. He saw the Japanese woman behind him holding a twenty-franc note in readiness for her orange juice and chocolate. He turned away to tear one of those thin plastic bags from a roll and was surprised to find them strong enough to hold three cartons of milk.

When he had packed them away, he heard the Japanese woman saying to the young man at the till: "I gave you a twenty."

"Ten," said the cashier.

"No, twenty," said the Japanese woman.

"Ten," said the cashier, "you get 6.20,"

The Japanese woman retrieved the change and was about to give in when Rusterholz said: "It was twenty. Give her another ten francs at once."

The assistant looked him up and down in surprise, and then said cheekily: "She gave me ten."

"She gave you twenty!" Rusterholz shouted so that everybody in the cramped shop turned towards him. "And I'm going to stand here until you give her the ten francs change."

The young man was insistent. "It was a ten she gave me," he maintained.

"Listen," said Rusterholz, "any cashier worth his salt doesn't put the note into the till before handing out the change. That's what this clip here is all about." And with one hand, he raised the clip for holding the notes and released it with a thwack against the till. "Only con men operate tills like that. I saw it was a twenty franc note."

The assistant placed both of his hands on his chest and shook his head vehemently. A man standing behind him, who obviously was his boss, put his hand on his shoulder and said: "Give her ten francs, Dragan."

"But—"

"Did you hear?"

With an extremely pained expression, the cashier handed over the ten francs to the Japanese woman.

He gave Rusterholz a piercing look as he left the shop red in the face.

The Japanese woman followed him out and said: "Thank you. I did give him twenty."

"It's alright," said Rusterholz. "I saw it, luckily. I feel sorry for you."

"It's okay," said the Japanese woman, smiling. "Thanks."

Rusterholz waved goodbye and started on his way home.

It was then he noticed that his knees were trembling and that he was breathing more rapidly. He had never done anything like this before. He had not hesitated for a second before intervening. He simply could not bear the way this frail little woman was being cheated. Although he had not seen the note being handed over himself, but only saw the woman as she was preparing to do so, he was convinced that the Japanese woman was telling the truth and had not just exchanged her twenty note for a ten at the last moment.

At supper he told his ten-year-old son Philipp about the episode on the pedestrian crossing and made him promise not to cross on red, and under no circumstances on a skateboard. "Yeah," said the boy, but it did not sound completely convincing.

When the boy had gone to bed and Rusterholz was drinking a glass of wine with his wife, Olivia, he told her about the incident in the railway station shop.

She was amazed. "Well, you've been quite the hero today then. I hope it isn't going to your head."

Charles laughed and said a little admiration from her

didn't come amiss and that the whole thing had amounted to rather more than he might have wished.

"Did you note the assistant's name?" his wife asked. He paused for a moment.

"The other man called him Dragan."

"He comes from Eastern Europe then," she said.

"It seems so," he replied.

"Be careful," said Olivia. "They're not to be trifled with."

Charles was a little startled but didn't show it.

In the next few days, he had a lot of work because he had the extra task of editing the new Paris leaflet for a sick colleague. It really wasn't his field, and he was annoyed at the repetitive vocabulary that was used to promote the hotels: comfortable, tasteful, stylish, well appointed, exceptionally quiet, and charming. It probably really meant there was a breakfast room in a basement with strip lighting and a morning quiz show on television. He had almost forgotten about the episode in the station shop when one morning he was reminded of it. He was just about to go down the steps at the suburban station to take the commuter train into town when he encountered the dark gaze of a young man, leaning against the upper section of the staircase. He must have been the shop assistant with whom he had had the disagreement, and Rusterholz was almost certain that the man had recognised him. Coming out of the underpass and going up the stairs to platform 5, he glanced back and saw the young man slowly following him. The train came in; Rusterholz got on with the crowd and lost sight of the man but he had misgivings until he reached his place of work in town.

It was a beautiful day, so when he got home in the evening he put on his tracksuit to go running on the sports field and in the small woods nearby. Usually he did some laps around the 250 metre track and then made for the woods shared with dog owners, families with children and picnickers, and circled around the woods on the two tracks that crossed them before returning to the sports field. When today he ran past the family play area, he heard some throaty voices shouting after him: "Go, go swissy!"

When he glanced round at them he saw a group of idle young men standing around the swings. One of them was swinging to and fro. The man on the swing was the same one who had followed him earlier that day, and again he gave him a piercing look. Rusterholz increased his pace, and instead of completing the round, he left the woods on the other side so that he returned home by going behind the school. When he rounded the bend to the school building, he got the impression that three of the young men had taken off running. This prompted him not to go home by the direct route, but to go a long way round via the neighbouring street. When he opened the gate to the tiny front garden, nobody from the group was to be seen.

His wife was surprised that he was home already, and he just mumbled that he hadn't been so keen to go running as he had thought.

During supper, Olivia told him that she had heard from a neighbour that all the sales staff at the railway station shop had been replaced. Only Swiss were working there now.

"That's very good for the Japanese customers," said Charles, laughing. Now he knew why he had seen Dragan twice that day. It was clear that he had been dismissed and it didn't look as if he had found any more work.

Rusterholz slept badly that night. No doubt all the staff had been replaced. However, it was possible to make a direct connection between him and the dismissal of the young salesman. He had not given any thought to the outcome when he spoke up for the Japanese woman. He knew that the situation on the job market was not favourable and it was even less so if you had a Slavic name. Recently, a school leaver with excellent grades had explained on television how he had applied by phone for a job that had been advertised, but when he gave a name ending in čić he was informed that the job had already been taken. A little later he applied again for the same job but disguising his voice and using a Swiss name, Mörgeli or Oetterli or Lutz, and was immediately asked for an interview. That was the mood in the country. Dragan would not find it easy and it was inevitable that he bore him a grudge. He would probably overlook the fact that it was his own fault because he had tried to cheat. Rusterholz again considered the possibility that he might have been mistaken because he had not witnessed the moment when the note was handed over.

This would mean that the Japanese woman had tried to deceive the assistant and he didn't think her capable of doing that. But Dragan? Yes, he was capable of that, for sure. At three in the morning Charles got up quietly, went into the kitchen and heated up some water. He opened the container of tea, thought for a moment what would be most likely to calm him down and took out a camomile tea bag.

"Are you ill?" said Olivia who was standing at the kitchen door in surprise.

"I can't sleep", said Charles. "This is the second time I've woken up."

"Is something troubling you?" asked Olivia.

"Not really," said Charles. "I can't explain it."

When Rusterholz walked to the station the next morning, Dragan was standing alone at the same spot, glanced at him only once and spat on the floor. Pretending not to see him, Rusterholz avoided going by him and took the second of the two staircases. As he headed for the stairs to platform 5, he turned round and saw that the man was not following him. Relieved, he took the train to the main station and during the short ride flicked through the free newspaper. A Russian who had lost his wife and two children in a plane crash had located the Swiss air controller he thought was guilty and had stabbed him. "Vengeance," said Rusterholz to himself. "They go in for vengeance in the East."

When he stepped off the escalator from the underground station into the large station concourse, Dragan was standing there and was just exchanging greetings with two friends, the palms of their hands meeting in a high-five style. Like him, they were both wearing black leather jackets and caps pulled down over their foreheads. Dragan briefly looked round, and Rusterholz passed behind a group of Japanese tourists with their Samsonite cases. He made for the exit on the left, although he usually used the main one.

A little later, he was sitting in the tram, certain that nobody was pursuing him, his brow covered with perspiration. How was it possible that Dragan had been waiting for him at the main station just like in the fable of the hare and the hedgehog? Rusterholz had got into the rear of the train, and if Dragan had run through the underpass and travelled in the front carriage, he would have got out first and rushed immediately up the escalator into the concourse, where his friends were already waiting for him. It was feasible, but hardly likely.

He found it an effort to concentrate on his work that afternoon. He had to obtain a series of quotations, and unable to spend time on any one area, had to keep a check list of priorities. He jumped all over Europe on the phone, speaking with business partners in England and France who would not dream of using any other than their own language.

Meanwhile, he negotiated with two hotels on a holiday island in Croatia where he dealt with obliging people who spoke very good German. Why, he thought, do we have so many grim types from the Balkans here, if they are all so friendly over there?

Why do we have so many foreigners here anyway? What do they all want? Can't they just be tourists here like we are over there? He had grown up in a village where there were two foreigners in his class: an Italian and a Spaniard. Now his son was in a class where there were just two Swiss; all the others were foreigners from all over the world and there wasn't even an Italian amongst them. Of course he was well aware that incomprehensible languages were the only ones to be heard at construction sites, and when he went to visit his grandmother in the nursing home, all the nurses pushing the old people around and caring for them were smiling Asians. This inevitably meant also that the three large chess games in the market square were firmly in the hands of people from the Balkans. Why was the second-hand car business that had been established on the former foundry site run by blacks? Besides, why were the blacks all so damn well dressed and their wives always pushing the latest prams? Who was paying for it all? He had noticed more than once when travelling by tram that he was the only Swiss, and it shocked him each time. The leaflets from his travel agency extolled the melting pots of New York or São Paulo, but Rusterholz had not yet managed to take any pleasure in Zurich as a melting pot.

At midday he intended to snatch a sandwich at the standing café in the parallel street. Turning the corner, he glanced quickly at his watch and turned around as if he had forgotten something, because he had seen Dragan with his two friends at the small table next to the entrance. He almost darted sideways along the streets and pavements until he was at the Paninoteca where Tamils sold baguettes au gratin; he bought one filled with cheese and spinach, paid for a mineral water as well, and then zigzagged his way to the office again.

In the evening it was not his wife who asked him what was the matter, but he asked her, because he saw immediately that something was troubling her.

"There's been an anonymous phone call," she said. She had said her name. The caller hadn't said anything for a bit and then hung up. Charles asked whether it could have been a wrong number.

Olivia said she didn't think so. She had a feeling that it was deliberate.

Sexual harassment?

No, but she said she had heard the other person breathing.

A man?

Yes, definitely. And street noises. It was either from a mobile or a public phone.

"The bastard," said Charles.

"Do you know who it is?"

"99% certain," said Charles, and then he told her that Dragan had been following him since he had been dismissed from the railway station shop.

"But he hasn't threatened you directly, has he?"

"No, but he is making it clear that he is out for me."

She asked him if he had tried to speak to Dragan.

He said he didn't think that very wise, especially when Dragan had two others with him.

"Are you afraid?" Olivia asked.

"Am I afraid? I don't know, but it certainly isn't a pleasant feeling."

Olivia suggested approaching Dragan and speaking to him the next time he saw him alone. Perhaps he only wanted to hear Charles say he was sorry that Dragan had been fired.

Alright, said Charles, he would do that, but only if Dragan were alone. He didn't relish being beaten up. And he warned her to take care, as they had to assume that he knew where they lived and who they were.

Take care, but how?

When somebody rings twice at the door, don't press the buzzer immediately, but first look down from the window and see if it is really the postman. And when leaving the house or returning, check that Dragan is not standing nearby. When he described to her what Dragan looked like, Olivia said that quite a number of people looked like that. That may be, thought Charles, but she would recognise him at once from his piercing gaze.

After supper, Philipp was impatient to play a game of chess with his father because he had been playing against the computer in the afternoon. Charles was so lacking in concentration when he played that he lost against his son for the first time. Philipp was jubilant and Charles said that next time he wouldn't stand a chance.

"Daddy, why are the Yugos always fighting?" Philipp asked him, setting the pieces out again.

"Are they?" Charles asked.

Yes, in their class; they had waited for Ramon in the underpass and beaten him up.

"But why?" Charles asked.

Ramon was shouting out that all Yugos were gay.

Charles told him not to call them Yugos; it was pejorative, and Ramon had been rather stupid. It was like Serbs or Croats or Bosnians shouting out that all Spaniards were womanisers.

"They do that too," said Philipp.

Charles sighed. It was never a good thing, he said, to say to other people that because they belonged to a particular nation they automatically behaved in a certain way. That implied that other people were not regarded as human beings, and there was one word for that, which he had without doubt heard before.

"Racism," said Philipp and beamed.

"Exactly," said his father moving his pawn to e4.

"And racism isn't good", said Phillip, countering by moving his to e5.

"No, certainly not. Racism can lead to war."

"Isn't chess really racist?" Phillip went on to ask.

"What makes you think that?"

"Because whites are playing blacks."

Charles couldn't help laughing and then thought how easy it was to explain to a child that racism is not good, and how difficult it is to behave accordingly.

Next morning Dragan was already standing on the platform when the commuter train arrived. Rusterholz looked him in the eye and made in his direction, but Dragan was getting on. Rusterholz ran to the same door, got in too, and went through both levels without finding him. People were so crowded together in front of the doors to the next carriages that he finally gave up. He could not see any sign of Dragan at the main station.

He saw him again only as the tram arrived. There he stood with his friends at the back, and as the tram departed without Rusterholz getting on, Dragan gave him his piercing gaze from the tram.

Again Rusterholz tried to imagine which direction Dragan might have taken. He had to tell himself that, although improbable, it was possible for Dragan to disappear if he had run immediately through the back entrance of the station to the nearby tram stop.

Rusterholz walked from the station to his place of work, not choosing the route the tram followed.

That evening he took the precaution of sitting in the first class for the journey home and was annoyed with the four girls who sat laughing in a compartment when it was obvious that they did not have first-class tickets. Young people were doing this more and more, hoping there would not be a check. But they didn't need to disturb other passengers. Rusterholz considered telling them off until he realized he was himself also travelling without a first-class ticket.

In the evening, he took a short walk with Olivia and Philipp in the nearby park. There was a pond there where they fed their stale bread to the ducks from time to time and Philipp had suggested doing that today.

Having fed the 'wild beasts', as Olivia playfully called them, they sat down on some stones on the bank, and Philipp tried to reach some leaves swimming near the bank with a stick.

"Look," Charles said quietly to Olivia. "He's sitting over there."

"Who?"

"Dragan. He is the middle one of the three."

Three young men with leather jackets were sitting on the other side of the pond, their caps pulled low over their foreheads.

One of them was using his mobile and Dragan was looking in their direction, as if by chance.

"Well," said Olivia, "I've seen him. Shall we go?"

They immediately left. Philipp wanted to stay and asked his father on the way to the tram whether Dragan was a Yugo.

"Don't say Yugo!" Charles snapped at him so severely that Philipp winced and became silent.

When Olivia had put her son to bed, Charles told her about that morning's episode and how unhappy he was that

Dragan had seen all three of them together. Then he asked her whether somehow they ought to warn Philipp.

Olivia was not sure, and the next morning, after Charles had gone to work, she reminded Philipp in a general way about not going along with strange men.

Philipp said he knew that already and asked whether she was mentioning that because of the three Yug—, because of the three men who were sitting at the pond yesterday.

"If you would really like to know; yes, one of them is probably angry with Daddy."

"Dragan, the one in the middle," Philipp concluded.

"Then you do know all about it," his mother said.

"Of course," he replied. "It was because of Dad he was thrown out of the shop."

Not a day passed when Dragan wasn't evident in some way. Either he was waiting for Rusterholz at the station in the suburb or at the main station, or he was sitting near the door in the standing café in town, or he appeared when school was out and gave Philipp one of his piercing looks. Philipp now recognized Dragan and told his parents every time he saw him. When asked whether he had been threatened in any way, Philipp said he hadn't; he was just standing on the opposite side of the street. When another anonymous telephone call came, Olivia used his name and told him just to say what he had against her, but they were cut off without a word having been spoken.

When Rusterholz saw Dragan, he was mostly in the

company of one or two of his friends, and if he was alone he managed to avoid direct contact.

They had already considered whether they ought to go to the police, but had been reluctant up till now. It was mainly Charles who found that too dramatic and was afraid the police would laugh at them. Dragan hadn't shown any inclination to attack him. Could you prevent anybody standing at the station or at the edge of the road? The most unnerving thing was that he knew their son, and Olivia often arranged it so that at the end of the lessons she was near the school without giving the impression that she was fetching Philipp, because he didn't want that. Besides, she hoped it would all stop as soon as Dragan found a new job.

About three weeks later Rusterholz received an anonymous call at his office. He immediately spoke to Dragan and told him he would report him if he didn't stop making himself a nuisance. Afterwards, very upset, he hung up when the phone changed to the engaged signal and decided to go to the police station after work.

Coming out of the station in the suburb, he heard some extremely strange music. At first he thought it was a carnival group, but it was much too early for that. Also it sounded too well organised. There was something quick, cutting and agitated about it. Brass instruments were spurred on by a kettle drum as if a squadron of Janizaries were moving through the area. He went to Market Square where the noise was coming from, walked past the chess players and noticed a Serb playing with an Indian wearing a turban. The Indian, sensing victory, was smiling while the Serb was in close conversation with his assistant. Now a group of musicians came slowly from a side street onto the square. Rusterholz approached them and stopped, fascinated by the zippy music which he couldn't place. There were men in dark, slightly shabby suits blasting their rhythms and melodies from trumpets and trombones. A man was walking alongside them, probably their leader or manager, distributing leaflets to passers by. Rusterholz took a few steps in his direction and was also handed a leaflet with the name of the orchestra on it and the venue where they were performing that evening. Rusterholz stood still, allowing the men with their instruments to go past, and he read once more on the leaflet the name, Orkestar Salijevic. When he raised his eyes again, Dragan was standing quite alone on the other side of the road looking over to him.

At first Rusterholz was about to go up to him, but suddenly he lacked the courage. How did he know that Dragan was not carrying a knife? He turned round and decided to make a detour to the police station. If Dragan followed him, he would have brought proof with him, so to speak. Dragan really did follow him, and suddenly Rusterholz was actually worried that he might do something to him before he reached the police station. He quickened his pace and reached a red traffic light. However, he crossed the tram lines and reached the island where there was the next red traffic light. Two delivery vans were waiting in the first lane in front of the pedestrian crossing. The second lane was free so that Rusterholz walked quickly over the road past the waiting cars and was caught up by a motorcycle and hurled through the air. He struck the ground in the middle of the crossing and was about to pull himself up, but something heavy prevented him from doing so.

When Dragan bent over him, his gaze had lost its piercing quality, instead he appeared deeply shocked. He held a handkerchief to Rusterholz's ear which turned immediately deep red.

Charles tried to catch his breath, but his lungs seemed to have holes in them. "Dragan," he said panting while the face above him was already blurring in front of his eyes. "What — do you want?"

Dragan placed his hand carefully under his head, bent down close to him and whispered:

"I am Mirko. Is there anything you want me to tell anybody?" ∘∘∘

The Clean-Up

A man came into a laundry and brought a pair of trousers that were in need of a thorough cleaning, as they were completely black with dirt. When he returned to pick them up, the sales lady gave him a plastic bag and told him that this was all that was left of his trousers.

"But it's empty!" said the man.

"Yes," said the sales lady, "but at least we got rid of this horrible filth."

"You're right," said the man. He took the bag, paid the bill, and left. ₀₀₀

The Farm Hand

Someone knocked on the door at Melchior Zinsli's mountain farm just as it was getting dark on a lovely summer evening. This surprised him. His farm was in a very remote region and it didn't happen very often that someone knocked on his door. His surprise diminished when he saw who it was at his door: it was the Pope.

"I welcome you," said Zinsli. "Please come in. You're arriving at just the right time."

"Yes," said the Pope in good German. "When I heard the weather report yesterday, I thought, it's now or never."

"Are you alone?" asked Zinsli, looking out in front of the house before he closed the door behind his guest.

"Yes," the Pope said. "It was not so easy, but I have a friend in the Swiss Guard who helped me."

He took his little white cap off and was relieved to put it on the sitting room table.

Melchoir Zinsli did not have any further questions. He asked the Pope to take a seat and set the table right away with strong coffee and warm milk, bread and Alpine cheese. The Pope did justice to the food and soon wanted to go to bed. He was pleased when he saw the farm hand's small room with the heavy bed and the large checkered bedspread. Since the Pope had arrived without any luggage,

Zinsli spontaneously offered him an old but clean night-shirt, and for the next day a pair of farm pants and a military shirt like most farmers wear in this area.

"What time are we getting up?" asked the Pope before getting into bed.

"I have to be with the cows at five o'clock, but it's early enough if I wake you at half past six."

"Glorious," said the Pope, brushing his right hand over the bedspread. "An hour later than at the Vatican."

The next morning he had slept well and long enough when Melchior Zinsli opened the door a little to let the aroma of coffee into the room. The first rays of sunlight were shining through the window and it promised to be a wonderful day.

Melchior Zinsli had planned to bring in the hay, and that was the reason he had written a letter to the Pope. He had read in The Agriculturist, a newspaper for farmers, that the Pope had referred to himself in an address to a European Union delegation of farmers as a farm hand for humanity. So Zinsli sat down and wrote that he had to do all the farming alone at his mountain farm and needed urgently a farm hand, especially when it was time to bring in the hay and asked the pope if he couldn't come to help for two, three days. He drew a little sketch of where his farmhouse could be found.

So now the Pope walked behind Melchior Zinsli and his Rapid mower all day, spreading the grass as it was cut. The next day they raked it into magnificent stacks, and the third day they loaded the stacks onto a hay loader and forked it all into the hay blower to get it into the barn. During breaks they ate rye bread and dried Alpine beef, drank fermented pear juice and chatted together about everything under the sun.

When the three days were over, the neighbouring farmers across the valley wondered where Melchior, who was not known to be the quickest, had suddenly found a farm hand, and quite a capable one at that. The Pope had rosy cheeks like 'Berner Rosen' apples. He had not read mass during this time, not to mention his breviary. But when saying goodbye to Melchior Zinsli, he told him he had never before had such a feeling of doing something so sensible as in the last three days, and Zinsli should write to him if he needed help again. Next year he would like to drive the Rapid mower himself, as it made such a nice rattling noise.

Then he climbed into the air rescue helicopter that the Swiss Guard had organized, and waved as it flew off heavenwards until it was a tiny point between the Beverin and Bruschghorn mountain peaks. Melchior Zinsli was deep in thought when he returned to his farmhouse, and the same evening he wrote a letter to a marriage bureau. He had no doubt that the Holy Father would accept another invitation, but it became clear to him that in the long run, he could not depend on help of this kind. He wouldn't invite the Pope again anyway because the one who is in charge of the Rapid mower is the boss, not the farm hand. ooo

The Open Refrigerator

A man searched for a raspberry yoghurt in his refrigerator but didn't find one. Disappointed, he left the kitchen, forgetting to close the fridge.

No matter how much the fridge was running, inside it kept getting warmer until after a while a small stream was dribbling out from under it.

"This is unbearable," moaned the hazelnut yoghurts.

"Is this a refrigerator or a stove?" grumbled the pork sausages.

"How are we supposed to stay fresh?" groaned the Emmental cheese, dripping from all its holes.

"I've had enough," said the natural yoghurt. "I'm leaving!"

"Where are you going?" asked the little sausages.

"Out into nature," said the natural yoghurt.

"I'm coming with you," called out an organic crispy-head lettuce.

"So are we!" yelled the hazelnut yoghurts, the pork sausages, the Emmental cheese, the butter and the two cartons of milk, and also the eggs and tomatoes nodded determinedly. A beer that was foaming in rage also joined them. Only the pickles, the little pearl onions and the olives stayed in their jars and daftly and lethargically gawked at the others.

They all hopped out of the fridge and, led by the natural yoghurt, walked in a line like a small, wet caravan into the living room. Soon they reached the potted palm tree next to the sofa.

"There!" the natural yoghurt called out. "Let's enjoy ourselves here in the shade of this palm tree."

They all sat down on the carpet under the potted palm tree and enjoyed the view of the arms of the sofa, the chair legs, the glass coffee-table and the television set. They made wet spots everywhere they sat. It wasn't long until the Emmental cheese said, "Whew! I'm so hot."

"Yeah," said the little sausages, "it's no cooler here than it was in the fridge." Big drops were running over the texts written on the milk cartons.

"Comrades!" the yoghurt called out, "let's get out of this house!"

They all got up, went downstairs together and out the door and then stood in the street. As it was summertime, heat engulfed them.

"It's warmer than inside a cow," said one of the milk cartons to the other. "I'm sweating," shouted the crispy-head lettuce. "I'm melting," whispered the butter. "We're getting blubbery," said the eggs. The tomatoes were getting red and the beer foamed silently to itself.

"Okay," said the natural yoghurt, "then let's go back to the fridge." But behind them, the door had closed and so they stood not knowing how to get in or how to stay out. Just then, the man who had gone to the dairy shop to get a few raspberry yoghurts returned and met up with almost the entire contents of his refrigerator in front of the door to his house.

"What are you doing here?" he asked them, surprised.

"We're just getting a bit of fresh air," mumbled the natural yoghurt.

"We're surely allowed to do that," snapped the pork sausage saucily, and all the others looked embarrassed at the ground.

"Okay then," said the man, and packed the yoghurts, the Emmental, the sausages, the eggs, the tomatoes, the crispy-head salad, the butter, the milk and the beer in his bag, carried them in, placed them one after the other into the refrigerator and closed the door. Soon, marvellously cool whiffs of air surrounded our adventurers. The butter breathed a sigh of relief, the sausages looked fresh again in their packaging, and the Emmentaler cheese beamed from every hole.

The pickles poked fun at them: "So, was it nice out in the open?" And the olives and the pearl onions giggled stupidly.

The yoghurts, the cheese, the sausages, the tomatoes, the eggs, the crispy-head salad, the butter, the cartons of milk and the beer all yelled at the same time, "Yes it was!"

And they all kept talking about the potted palm tree, the stairway, and the heat outside the front door until they were eaten or drunk. ooo

The Recapture

One day as I was sitting at my desk and looking out the window, I saw on the TV antenna of the house across the street an eagle. I have to say that I live in Zurich and that in this country, eagles live only in the Alps. The closest is maybe in the mountains of the canton of Glarus about fifty kilometres away. All the same, I was sure this was an eagle. Its impressive size and the provocative way it held its head reminded me of the stuffed bird on display in the school building of my youth. We always passed it on our way to the gym and there on a cardboard sign was written 'Golden Eagle'. I was sure that it was an eagle sitting there on the antenna of the neighbour's house. Perhaps, I thought, it had escaped from the zoo or from an aviary, but then it crossed my mind that usually these birds' wings were clipped so that they could do no more than make a few futile hops. Then I thought it had perhaps got lost? That can happen to an animal too. But immediately I felt this could not have happened to the animal over there. It also struck me as strange that it would just sit on one of those houses. We used to live in the country, and it always irritated me that the buzzards circling up high never came to our garden to eat the mice. I was told then that buzzards were shy about getting near houses. They also stayed away from the pole that I put up for them far from the house. Not once over the years had one of them dared to fly down. And now an eagle was sitting across the street on the rooftop, surrounded by other rooftops, and was looking down at the street with its head cocked slightly sideways, and nobody seemed to take notice of it.

I decided to fetch my wife and went downstairs to the family flat to get her. But when we got back, the eagle had disappeared. I thought I saw it circling high up over Hotel International that can be seen from our flat. But my wife was right when she said it could have just as well been a buzzard or even a gull.

It came back a few weeks later accompanied by an-other eagle, and together they started to build a nest on the most hidden part of the neighbour's roof, between the base of the antenna and the chimney on a small cupola. The neighbours didn't know how they should react and just left them alone. Within a short time the eagles had built their eyrie in which one of them was sitting while the other was out hunting for mice, squirrels and kittens.

Of course the birds caused quite a stir, especially since it turned out that they were not the only ones. From all over town there were reports of newly built eagle nests. The ornithological association provided a listing of them, and kept it up-to-date. Biologists were busy trying to find out why these rare animals had suddenly changed their habits, and they were unable to find an explanation. They said that normally no living being in the animal kingdom changes its habitat so quickly. People were advised to protect their small pets, keep dogs on a leash if possible and not let guinea pigs and rabbits run freely outdoors. Furthermore the city officials decided to be tolerant of the eagles since it turned out that they were also preying on rats, of which there are more than enough in our city.

You soon got used to suddenly having an eagle landing on the ground next to you, biting a stray cat to death, when a new incident made people uneasy.

One morning at a traffic light at Bellevue, one of the busiest and most congested crossings in the centre of Zurich, deer stag antlers were found. There was hardly a doubt that these antlers had been shed by the deer that very night. And they weren't just any antlers, but these had twenty-four branches on them. An enquiry at the Swiss Game Wardens showed that the largest known deer lived in the region of Beverin and its antlers had twenty-two branches. Beverin is in the Canton of Grisons and the deer belong to those animals that have almost completely withdrawn from the Swiss lowlands over the course of the last century. But since nobody had observed this deer shedding its antlers, and it was not seen anywhere in the next days and weeks either in the city or in the surrounding forests, it was assumed that someone must have found the antlers in the mountains and, obviously not aware of their value, had recently just dropped them at Bellevue.

Therefore nobody expected what happened about three months later on one of the first days of summer. An early morning stroller called the police at 4 a.m. to report that a number of deer had gathered in the park near Bürkliplatz and were blocking the footpaths. Two police-men sent out to check on this, confirmed it and set off a major alert. They saw that there were not only individual deer moving among the bushes, but that it must be a whole herd: the number was difficult to ascertain, but there could easily have been hundreds of them. The park is bordered on one side by the lake and on the other by two broad streets. So after consulting the director of the zoo, the police de-cided to block off the park so that they could catch the ani-mals individually or shoot them. In great haste rolls of elec-tric fencing, the kind used for herds of cows, were brought to the scene. At about 7 a.m., when the morning traffic be-gan to roll in, the whole park had multiple, electrically charged fences surrounding the deer, who peacefully and steadily made munching sounds as they chewed away the grass, flower beds, and the foliage on the trees. As official-dom was pondering what to do, a huge animal across from the Kongresshaus pushed the wires up high with its antlers and tore them apart in one heave without hurting itself in any way. This was the animal with the twenty-four branch antlers that was now at the front of the whole herd trotting on the street towards Bellevue.

Nobody knew how to cope with these deer. Sharp-shooters were called in. Game wardens and gamekeepers came too, but shooting the deer in the midst of the crowded streets was out of the question. And the deer were present only in crowded streets. They walked across Bellevue with the police and cars behind them and strolled leisurely down the Limmatquai along the river.

Confusion reigned. Trams couldn't move and their passengers didn't have the courage to disembark. Drivers tried to steer their cars on the sidewalks. Some of them left their cars in the middle of the street as they saw the deer approaching and fled to the entrances of buildings. Others rolled up their windows and stayed in their cars. They disappeared in the herds of animals like a stone in the floods. A strange silence accompanied the whole procession. Everywhere motors were turned off and only the sliding and scraping of the hundreds of hooves on the asphalt could be heard. From time to time a window broke or a car got scratched, but people kept quiet as church mice. Policemen ran in front of the herd, trying to warn people. The zoo director advised them to avoid using loudspeakers to prevent setting off panic among the deer, since what they feared most of all was that the herd would stampede. It was hoped the deer would find a way out of town and into one of the forests in the region. But they didn't. The animals chose a route that looked more like a tour of the city. At Central, they made a sharp right turn into Niederdorf and left it at Predigerplatz. Then, after eating away the scant greenery at the Pfauen, they turned right again down Rämistrasse to cross Bellevue a second time, after which they didn't head for the Uetliberg as everyone had hoped but turned right again at the Stadthausanlage to swing into Bahnhofstrasse.

At Paradeplatz the big banks barricaded their entrances. The jewellers and fur dealers let their rolling shutters clatter over their doors and looked fearfully out their shop windows at the brown beasts inexorably pushing along and entirely filling the streets

Already they were starting to close off the underpass at the railway station and pull down the huge protective grating at the Hauptbahnhof when the herd made a surprise right turn at the Modissa shop and headed towards the Rudolf-Brun Bridge. A little later — the first animals were just coming through under the bridge by the main police station — a heavy downpour suddenly brought the herd to a stop. The one with the twenty-four-branch antler, who was always at the front, paused for a moment, lifted its head high, looked around and headed in a slow trot towards the Urania Car Park, followed by all the other animals. That was an unexpectedly lucky development. As soon as the deer were inside, the entrance and exit to the multi-storey car park were barricaded by trucks to trap the animals inside.

The decision to shoot was made quickly. People who happened to be in the car park were summoned then through the loudspeaker system to remain without fail in their cars and to stay away from the entrance and exit gates. From the screams heard from the outside, obviously not everyone got the message. Then several soldiers with machine guns were posted across from the entrance and exit, reinforced by the best sharpshooters of the city corps. They waited until it stopped raining. Then the trucks drove away from the gates and a firecracker was thrown into the car park that made a loud blast. The detonation was effective. With a powerful leap, the deer with the twenty four branch antlers leapt from the third floor of the open spiralling ramp and the whole heard followed it in such a short time that the sharpshooters, who had to immediately change their position, were only able to shoot one or two deer. Using the machine guns was out of the question because the buildings at the Lindenhof were in the firing line. A single doe got lost in the lower level exit and was hit, along with a petrol pump, by a round of fire, so that the blood of the animal merged together with the petrol gushing from the pump, forming a reddish brown puddle.

Now, as if according to a plan, the herd split up in groups of three or two deer through the whole town. Many deer were also moving along on their own. The results of this morning were not good. Only eleven animals had been shot. It was estimated that there were at least thirty times as many animals. Besides, four people were injured in the parking garage. One of them, a woman, who had been trampled on by the deer, was in critical condition.

Since the deer didn't leave the city, or when they did, they returned shortly again, a special squad was formed to combat deer. That was a precarious undertaking, especially since shooting with firearms was rarely possible without endangering someone's life. For this reason, several men were sent to America where they were trained by cowboys on how to throw a lasso. But they were not successful in driving the deer out of town either. People simply got used to the sight of a deer dashing down a one-way street followed by a policeman on a horse swinging his lasso.

There is something to be said for that, indeed. And in a way, it enriched the lives of people in the city. But on the other hand, these animals brought fear with them. The screams of a cat struggling against the deathly attacks of an eagle is almost unbearable. On an autumn morning, if you are awakened from a deep sleep by the low and unrelenting mating calls of the deer that echo from walls of buildings like from cliffs, you remain awake the whole day. And wherever in town two deer charge against each other crackling their antlers together, the streets become immediately empty.

At any rate, the eagles and the deer stayed until autumn, and as winter set in, they just stayed on, even bringing new guests with them.

A deer was found on a foggy morning in the middle of the Hardturm stadium. Besides its hide and bones, only bloody entrails were lying there and the snow around it was all red.

At first people thought it had been attacked by dogs. But as the cantonal veterinarian saw the tracks, he was not so sure about it and had several biologists come to have a look. Together they studied the scene and announced their verdict. These tracks, said the cantonal veterinarian as the team of biologists behind him frowned bleakly at the ground, are from a wolf. And it can't be just one wolf, but it must be a pack of them.

It took a while until a wolf was sighted the first time. For a long time only their tracks were seen. Apparently they had it in for the deer, as the deer at the Hardturm stadium was not the only victim. Every two or three days an animal was found somewhere in town in a similar mess. The first to actually see the wolves were the children in my eight-year-old son's school class. One morning as his class was having its gym lesson sledding at the edge of the forest of the Käferberg, the wolves were suddenly there and attacked the boy standing the furthest at the back. He was the son of a Yugoslav. He screamed only once, said the teacher, who was beside herself in horror. Apparently the wolves had bit through the carotid artery in his throat. When the police arrived, they could only follow the trail of blood leading close to the pond in the forest. There lay all that the wolves had left of Ilja. The wolves, however, had disappeared and could not be tracked down by dogs that were sent out to look for them. They lost their scent at the Nordheim cemetery.

From now on a state of emergency reigned over Zurich. It wasn't proclaimed. It was just there. Schools, together with parents, started organizing for the children to go to school in groups accompanied by adults. Men conscripted in the army were given permission to accompany the children's groups with the triggers of their assault rifles cocked ready to shoot. My son was immensely disturbed by the event that had stricken his class. He calmed down a bit only once I bought him a large Boy Scout knife that I had until then not allowed him to have because I considered it too dangerous. He always carried this knife in his belt when he went with the other children to school. At school, by the way, a substitute teacher was giving the lessons because the teacher had suffered such a shock that she couldn't face teaching her class for weeks.

The public authorities made great efforts now to get this unusual situation under control. They had got used to the fact that every year a few children were run over and killed by cars. That was a possible way to die in the city. But that children are mauled to death by wolves is something that should not happen in a city like Zurich. Residents were called on to make suggestions that would be evaluated by an emergency task force. Hunting licence holders were given permission to shoot as many wolves as they could, as well as the eagles and the deer since it was clear by now that these events were all related. They instructed the hunting licence holders to shoot only when they were certain no human life was endangered.

After that the situation improved somewhat. In a short time more animals were hunted down than the special troops had been able to kill. And also, what they had hardly dared to hope for started happening quickly. They succeeded in luring the pack of wolves into a trap. A wounded deer had been placed at a dead-end street in the Friesenberg neighbourhood where they enticed it to stay by giving it plenty of feed. Sure enough, the whole pack showed up early in the morning and attacked the deer, enabling the machine gun marksmen positioned along the street and on the higher floors of the terraced houses to shoot the animals easily. Within a minute, thirty-three wolves with bloody snouts lay on the ground. Zurich breathed a sigh of relief. The forestry official whose idea this had been received hundreds of telegrams and calls congratulating him. In the evening the city was in a festive mood. Bars and restaurants stayed open all night, and in many restaurants they served free beer.

The next morning the airport had to be closed because of a half-eaten deer lying between the take-off and the landing runways. The investigation showed: it was wolves.

From then on people began slowly to get used to the fact that they might not be able to get rid of these animals, but would somehow have to live with them. Where they came from was not known. They were not reported missing from any place and no other town had been invaded by them, neither in Switzerland nor anywhere else in Europe. It affected only Zurich, and nobody knew why.

The first bear showed up in spring. It strolled through the underground passages to the railway station known as Shopville. It flipped over all the rubbish containers with a swat of its paw and sniffled through the debris for something edible. People fled up the escalators or pushed into the entrances of the shops. The bear helped itself generously from the displays of a big food shop. A member of the

Railway Security Corps shot it from behind as the bear was reaching for a melon. Rather taken aback, the animal fell to the floor, rolled over once before landing on its stomach and lying there like a bedside carpet.

Shortly after that we heard that in the Enge tunnel a bear had brought traffic to a standstill and disappeared upstream along the Sihl. It had been at least seventy years since the last bear was hunted in the Engadine mountain region, and suddenly the life of bears was an issue again and we had to be prepared to run into one in the middle of town. They were less dangerous than the wolves, for they never appeared in packs but usually trotted through the streets on their own. Nevertheless, you had to be careful, especially with small children. Immediately it was permitted to shoot bears. But they could not be eradicated.

On the whole, people remained calm when the bears appeared. Real panic only broke out among the townspeople when in Stauffacher Square, an elderly man reached into a newspaper rack and was bitten in his hand by a snake, a viper. In spite of getting immediate medical care, he died the same day. Several times that week, poisonous snakes popped out of the left-luggage lockers at the railway station and tried to bite people who wanted to remove their belongings. We heard about an Italian lady in the industrial district who found a viper when opening her breadbox and was bitten by it as she tried to kill it with a frying spatula. Almost everyone began to look under the bed before going to sleep. We always threw the bed covers completely back first because we had heard the warning that snakes preferred warm spots. At my five-year-old son's kindergarten, a tessellated snake was found in a toy chest. The janitor killed it immediately. Afterwards it turned out that it had not been poisonous, but after this incident we started thinking about whether we should take our children to my brother's in Olten. Many parents took their children out of school and took them somewhere else. A number of families moved away entirely. Apartments in the surrounding towns became even harder to find than before. And as early as April, the campgrounds in the entire lowland region were full to bursting

All the same, we decided to stay. It was around this time that I heard that carnivorous birds were turning up that had never been seen in Switzerland before — a bird of prey that ate only snakes. I hoped it would be helpful in diminishing this new threat. But there wasn't the slightest sign of this, and it turned out that there was another threat lying in wait over the city to make us even more helpless. It looked harmless at first, even promising, but soon it became clear that this was precisely what could finish us off.

This threat came from plants, especially from two varieties. The first was ivy that suddenly started growing incredibly fast. During a single night it could grow from a garden to the middle of the road, and if it was cut in the morning it was already at the edge of the sidewalks by the evening. With a huge effort every day, it was possible to prevent it from clinging to glass and concrete buildings, to administration buildings of large firms, to hotels, banks and shops. They all had to hire people who did nothing else all day but cut ivy. And after the ivy, other climbing plants, knotweed, clematis, wisteria and other decorative parasites started intermingling with the ivy to take on the battle for the streets, buildings and subways.

At the same time a second type of plant appeared in a size never seen before and that was only known from swampland. I don't know whether you are familiar with butterbur, a meaty plant with huge leaves that is found in the mountains along streams or growing in wet cracks. This plant shot up suddenly out of the lawns, and the leaves were so big that they could cover a parked car. Scouring rushes reached the height of birch trees, and ferns bent from one side of the street to the other so that you could easily walk under them. In spite of their pliability, these plants were so strong that they stole all nourishment from the other plants. Sturdy trees dried out in a short time, and some fell down in gusts of wind so that now the townsfolk stay at home whenever there is a change in the weather. We only go out when it is necessary because, as you can imagine, this vegetation is more conducive for wolves, snakes, bears and deer than it is for human beings. And now that so many streets are closed because they are completely overgrown, and people have to hack a path through them with bread knives and hatchets, you can no longer depend on being rescued if you are attacked by a wild animal. That's why we are becoming more and more self-reliant and taking care of ourselves. Often, days go by before we hear from the authorities or meet the police on patrol. At the same time, there is a new feeling for neighbourliness that comes from everybody being desperately dependent on each other. Yet there is a new form of robbery and plundering since there is hardly an authority that we can rely upon for life's needs. People start mistrusting each other and it has happened that people who are fighting their way through an ivy path outside their own neighbourhood get shot by the escorts of a group of children.

Now it is almost autumn and nobody knows how things will continue. Of the few trains that can still move on the tracks in the middle of the main railway station, those that are leaving are full, their baggage cars overflowing with suitcases and bags tied with string, whereas there is hardly anyone on the incoming trains. As for the motorways, only those access roads that go out of town are kept open. The incoming ones have long since been buried under metres of green foliage.

People are hoping that when the plants wilt they won't grow as fast, and an extensive clearance and eradication project can be started. But I have my doubts about its success. From the beginning the herbicides applied in almost irresponsible quantities turn out to be ineffective. Ivy also stays green in winter and we can already see that the stem of the scouring rush is no longer soft and pliable, but is more and more like tree bark. In any case, we don't really know what kind of a winter we'll have. The last one dumped unusually large masses of snow on us, and our heating oil tank is only a quarter full because the fuel trucks can no longer get through our street. Anyway, I've sawed up the pear tree that collapsed next to a giant fern, and I'm prepared to spend the cold days with the family in my study which has the only wood stove in the house.

When I look out the window of this study, I can still see between the tops of the scouring rushes eagles taking off and landing on the neighbour's roof, and pulling apart still twitching pieces of meat and pushing them in the beaks of their pitifully screeching brood. At the same time the Hotel International stands on the horizon like a massive old tree trunk, completely covered by the clinging ivy, from which protrude blue and white clematis and knotweed blossoms. Recently, some little capuchins have appeared among them. You can follow the trail of their yellow and red blossoms up to the tenth floor.

Now all is quiet outside my window. The construction site of the new Migros market is deserted. The arm of the crane swings like a giant flower in the wind. The trams have stopped running. The nearest road that can still be used is out by the indoor swimming pool.

The house across the street is empty and I'm sitting here wondering if there is any point in leaving the city, or if it is all only the beginning of something that will spread from here unstoppably. ₒₒₒ

The Creation

In the beginning, there was nothing except God.

One day He received a vegetable crate full of peas. He wondered where it could have come from since He knew no one other than Himself.

He was rather dubious about the whole thing and just left the crate standing there, or rather, hovering there.

After seven days the pods burst, and the peas shot out into the void with great force.

Many of the peas that had been in the same pod stayed together and orbited around each other.

They began to grow and to give light, and in this way the void became the universe.

God was mystified by all of this. Later, all kinds of living creatures developed on one of the peas; some of them were humans who knew Him. They attributed to Him the creation of the universe and worshipped Him for it.

God did not dispute this, but to this day He is trying to figure out who the devil could have sent Him the crate of peas. ∘∘∘

The Cross-Country Skier

He tried to pick up speed. He assumed towards evening that he had escaped from the big group of skiers as he turned off the path out of the forest. But now, just as he was getting to the valley, he heard the familiar scrunching sounds behind him together with the slight clanking of the ski sticks being jabbed in the snow. It irritated him that at this time when most of them were heading for the meeting and starting points, someone had the idea to ski up the valley. It was already getting shadowy and the cross-country ski run went uphill. He needed perseverance if he wanted to continue at the speed he now skied at. He wanted to continue at that speed. He didn't want to let anyone pass him. He wanted to see the ski run unencumbered by other skiers in front of him, like now. He had taken up cross-country skiing because he wanted to dash through deserted space, and he was appalled by the crowds of people sprawling out over the two tracks. Overtaking was not always possible, just like on a road. Above all, the fact that this sport was also possible for older people — actually a positive aspect of this sport — somehow put him off when he saw how many half-mummified columns were shuffling with great effort from one little hill to the other, or when he skied downhill ploughing through the sweaty fumes of the elderly gasping for breath as they struggled uphill. That's exactly why he had made a turn and wanted under no circumstances for someone to overtake him, even if the scrunching sounds behind him were getting closer. He could not ski any faster. Actually, he always wondered how anyone could be faster than he was. He pushed harder with his poles, but it was quite painful to his left elbow and also to his hand due to his fall yesterday, but he didn't want to see anyone in front of him. It was beautiful here. The little stream on the left was almost frozen over and freshly fallen snow lay on the trees of the forest. He now began to sweat profusely. He opened his anorak during a brief downhill swing before making his ascent in a kind of hopping step he had become used to by imagining he was copying the style of a cross-country skier. At the same time it was getting colder and he felt how in different places his whiskers were being drawn together by clumps of ice. He was breathing heavily and his rival, though he didn't turn around to see him, must have been very close behind him. The fact that he could not pass him was heartening. The stone hut that marked the first third of the run was behind him. During the day one saw a lot of people resting there, but now it was deserted. Actually, he had intended to go only as far as the hut since it was getting dark quickly, but now he was in a race and he only wanted to give up once he had been overtaken. The tracks now ran through the forest which was almost dark. Here were also the first slopes that were so steep that he could not just ski straight up like the good skiers, who, unlike him, were also highly skilled in the art of waxing. It annoyed him that he had to struggle uphill with skis that had no sharp edges. He slid back two or three times, but his pursuer didn't seem to do any better. He found it difficult to find his rhythm again and contemplated stopping and letting his rival pass him. But then there was an open space, the run going slightly downwards, then the bridge over the stream, and he knew it was the halfway point of the valley, and he gained strength of mind to keep going. Shortly afterwards he realized he could not hold out much longer. The air was so cold that he almost had to cough, his hip hurt from his having constantly to push off, his elbow was burning and a sharp pain in both lungs wouldn't go away. He wanted to make it to the Alp huts, to both Alp huts that were so flat they seemed to be two bumps on the earth. The points of the skis of his enemy must now be right behind the ends of his skis. He could feel the movement of the skier behind him, hear how he thrust his poles into the snow and gasped like someone using his full force to reach him. Just ten more steps, five more, he mustn't let himself be passed, no, in his mind he had set the finish line at the Alp huts, just one step more. Yes, he had made it, he couldn't go on, no way. He stopped skiing, propped himself up with his armpits over both poles, looked back and saw that behind him there was no one

Only then did he collapse. ∘∘∘

The Whitsun Sparrow

The Whitsun Sparrow is not as well-known as the Easter Bunny. On Whitsunday he puts one little blade of grass on everybody's window sill, the kind of grass he uses to build his nest. But nobody ever notices this. Only sometimes a housewife who wipes it away immediately.

Year after year the Whitsun Sparrow flies into a rage about his lack of success and is envious of the Easter Bunny, but I also think the egg idea is better. ooo

The Name Change

One day I was standing, or to be precise sitting, in line to renew my passport, when I met a man who wanted to change his surname by adding an extra 'd'. This is the story he told me.

The village where he had grown up was also home to a monastery in front of whose gates babies were abandoned from time to time, as it was known that the monks would take them in, raise them and give them a good education. These foundlings, whose parents were unknown, were all given the surname Leuthart, a common name in the region. However, the respectable burghers of the area spelt the name with a dt at the end, Leuthardt, and so the d was dropped in order to distinguish the Leuthart-named foundlings from them.

The man who sat next to me was such a Leuthart, raised in the monastery until he came of age when he had emigrated to America. Now, having made his fortune as was right and proper, he had returned to Switzerland to enjoy his final years. But it now irked him that despite his fame and fortune, he still carried a pauper's name, and he had decided to submit an application to change it from Leuthart to Leuthardt.

This was easier said than done, as both of his sons and

their families had to be in agreement. He even needed his daughter's consent despite the fact that she was married and had taken her husband's name. As his sons were settled in America, they wouldn't hear of adding an extra d to a name that was not exactly anglophile to start with. His daughter, who was now called Rabinovitch and lived in Seattle, also failed to warm to this extra consonant. Her marriage was on the rocks and the addition of a d to her name was hardly likely to soften the blow of her pending divorce.

In such an exceptional case a special concession was required to restrict the change to one person only. The requirements were much stricter though. Among others, the milk brother, that is the boy with whom he was nursed, had to be sought and his permission obtained. Various notaries had to send confirmations and statements back and forth across the Atlantic, confirming that the new Leuthardt with a d was in fact the former Leuthart without a d and that he was really the father of his three d-less children. That way they couldn't be cheated out of their inheritance because a d had muscled its way into the family name.

A further stumbling block came from the village in which he had been raised. An old Leuthardt decided to appeal and block the change, seeing it as degrading to his name and fearing it would set a precedent for others to follow. Leuthart was not discouraged, for he had engaged another ruinously expensive lawyer to fight for his d. When I asked him if all of this trouble over a name was really worthwhile, he replied that he'd come this far and wasn't going to give up. He said that this business with the d had given his life a new purpose. To tell me the truth, he couldn't imagine what he would do with his time if one day he reached his goal and was no longer called Leuthart but Leuthardt. ooo

Kosovo, Yes

The indigenous people of our railway stations are foreigners. The more remote a place is, the more likely you are to find foreigners at the railway station. They pick up from the scent of the tracks and express trains a feeling of being connected, however faintly, to the country they've left and where they'd rather be, if a powerful and merciless hand had not grabbed them and plopped them down here of all places, in Flüelen, for example. I've just been visiting a classroom of children in the deeply snowed-in valley of Schächen nearby. I'm sitting in the station's waiting room, waiting for the train to Zurich.

As I'm searching in my bag for a book that I'm sure I had with me to read during the train ride, from the doorway I hear a delicate little voice with a greeting in mankind's original lingo: not "hello," not "hoi" or "salü" but a kind of utterance that means, "I'm here. Are you here too?"

I don't want to listen, and only after a while when I can't find my book, do I notice that a young boy is sitting at my side. He's small, skinny, pale. He catches my glance and repeats his utterance of greeting.

I ask him in Swiss German which train he's waiting for, to which he immediately produces the standard reply he keeps ready for all occasions: "No understand."

"Bosnia?" I ask.

He shakes his head.

"Kosovo?"

He nods vehemently and says: "Kosovo yes."

"*Miredita*," I say.

Recently, being confused by the many Albanians in our country, I had bought a book to learn the Albanian language. *Miredita* was the only word that I could remember so far. It means 'good day'.

The youngster smiles and asks hopefully: "Albanian?"

I shake my head. Our conversation tentatively comes to an end. He keeps watching me like someone who's sitting in the first row. The performance has only just begun.

"Is your mother here too?" I ask.

"Mother yes," he replies.

"Your father?"

"Father yes."

"How do you say 'mother' in Albanian?" I want to know. After all, I've got a living language lesson sitting in front of me.

But that's asking too much. "Mother no," he says meekly.

The complete breakdown of communication about to occur is prevented by the lad's leaning forward and tugging on my coat and saying "coat."

I confirm his declaration and tug on his jacket and say "jacket." By the way he repeats the word, I realize he already knows it.

I point to my shoes and he calls them "shoes," and then I try again and ask: "Shoes — Albanian?"

This time he understands what I want and says "Kepuce."

I repeat the word and he is pleased with me.

The wall is decorated with a fresco titled *Föhnwache* (storm alert), by Heinrich Danioth. Three grim-looking men in firemen's dress are standing at the shore of the lake. They are gazing at two female figures in dancing poses who are apparently depending on the firemen's protection should there be a storm.

We both look at the picture that I say is a "picture" and he repeats "picture."

That settles it. We're finished. I try to think of an easier topic of conversation. Why not learn a little bit more Albanian now that I've already found out what shoes are called?

"Mother — Albanian?" I asked again.

He shakes his head no, "Mother no." He's already told me that.

I don't give up. "Father — Albanian?"

"Father no."

Okay, if you say so. "What's your name? Your name?"

He gleams, "Martin."

Then he points to me. "You?"

"Franz," I say.

Then I get up and say "My train's arriving."

He's disappointed. Now that we know each other's names and are already almost friends, I go away and leave him sitting in Flüelen with mother no and father no.

I buy a newspaper at the kiosk and go to the platform of my train.

As I'm getting on the train, I see the young fellow standing in front of the kiosk. He waves at me as the train pulls away and I wave back.

I don't know anybody in Flüelen.

Nobody, except Martin. ∘∘∘

Intermission

During the intermission of a play in which actors with absurd make-up and in shimmering costumes were gesticulating wildly while reciting their parts and bumping into other actors wearing different make-up and making their entries in artistically tattered rags, in which abundantly or barely dressed actors got stabbed by candlesticks and theatrical swords, and in which in the end two actors in a far-away country, that was the stage, bathed in golden raindrops fluttering down from above — so, during the intermission of this play which was supposed to picture life as a whole, I drank a glass of orange juice and then stepped out into the fresh air or rather stood under the arcades outside the theatre's entrance where you can get some fresh air while standing with your back to a bookshop window and looking straight ahead towards the tram stop where it was drizzling.

After standing there for a while, alone among others, I saw a figure on the left of one of the arcade's columns dart past who I expected to appear again right away on the right of that column since it was moving in that direction. It must have changed its mind behind that column because it appeared again left of the column walking backwards and staring at the people in front of the theatre and also at the

brightly lit hall behind the big glass doors. This figure —
there was no doubt about it — this figure was an old
woman, a very odd little old woman.

She was walking with a cane, stooped almost at a
right angle, and was wearing a faded raincoat and a small
rain hat with its brim turned down, its original blue colour
barely recognisable. What seemed very odd was the little
white mask bound over her mouth. It was a kind of
surgeon's mask made of gauze with two bands on each
side, one going above and one below the ear. It bulged
suspiciously over her mouth and cheeks so one would
suspect a boil or some other hideous sore hiding under-
neath.

After staring motionlessly at the people, the old
woman continued walking in her original direction but she
stopped again just to the right of the column and stared
again, as if aghast, into the arcades. Then all of a sudden
she shoved her way through the crowd of theatregoers. She
was amazingly agile, perhaps because she was used to
people shrinking back from her. She almost crashed into
the bookshop window. First with her eyes wide open she
felt the window ledge with her hand as if to make sure that
it was really there, then from her right-angle stoop she
suddenly stood up straight like a meerkat sniffing around,
and then she fell back into her stooped posture.

When turning away from the bookshop window
through which the theatregoers could be seen behind the
bookshelves, she noticed a tram nearing the tram stop and

scooted off. Briskly and without bumping into anyone she dashed through the crowd and without looking left or right stepped onto the street holding her hand straight out, crossing in front of two cars screeching to a stop. Just as she reached the tram, the automatic doors closed. Had not a passenger inside the tram got up and pressed the button for the door to open, the tram would have left without her.

I saw her stumble up the steps of the tram and almost fall from the jolt of its moving on, and when the tram turned right and she saw that it was tram number 8 and realised she had taken the wrong one, she immediately struggled to her feet again, reaching for the button to open the door which she kept pressing incessantly but all to no avail. The tram slowly disappeared around the bend with the desperately masked old woman.

This episode was so strange that I wondered if it was part of the play. But after the intermission when the curtain opened again and two actors spoke to a king dressed entirely in gold, I realised that the strange old woman was not in any way involved in the production.

She was part of another play. ₒₒₒ

The Salesman and the Moose

Do you know the saying "Selling a gasmask to a moose?"

That's what Swedes say about a person who is very capable and smart; and I'd like to tell you where this saying comes from.

Once upon a time there was a salesman who was renowned for being able to sell just about anything to anybody. He had sold a toothbrush to a dentist, a loaf of bread to a baker and a crate of apples to an apple grower.

"Only when you can sell a gasmask to a moose are you a really good salesman," his friends told him.

So the salesman kept going north until he came to a forest where only moose lived.

"Good morning, you look like you need a gasmask," he said to the first moose he came across.

"What for?" the moose asked. "The air is very clean here."

"Nowadays, everybody has a gasmask," the salesman replied.

"I'm very sorry," the moose said, "but I don't need one."

"You just wait, sooner or later you'll need one," the salesman answered.

Soon afterwards he started building a factory in the middle of the forest where only moose lived.

"Are you crazy?'" his friends asked.

"No," he replied, "I just want to sell the moose a gasmask."

When the factory was built, its smokestack started emitting enormous amounts of poisonous fumes, so the moose went to the salesman and said, "Now I need a gasmask."

"See, I told you!" the salesman said and sold the moose a gasmask. "These are high-quality products," he said merrily.

"The other moose now also need gasmasks," the moose said. "Do you have some more in stock?"

"You're lucky," the salesman replied, "I still have thousands of them."

"By the way, "the moose said, "what do you produce in your factory?"

"Gasmasks," the salesman replied.

P.S. I'm not quite sure after all if this is a Swedish or a Swiss saying, but it doesn't really matter as these two countries often get mixed up anyway. ₒₒₒ

The Wild Chase on the Oberalp

In earlier times, around midnight and during a full moon, it might be experienced by a herdsman and scare the daylights out of him. Nowadays it can be experienced every Sunday if the weather is fine.

The most restless souls from the valley head for the mountain pass at the first rays of sunlight. Spellbound, they sit at the wheels of their cars as if possessed by a dark force that has propelled them out of their beds and pushed them relentlessly upwards toward the crossing of the pass summit before thundering down again on the other side. Whoever has glimpsed the pale faces behind the windshields, the tortured expression of the driver or the dull stare of the passenger, realizes that this ride was not undertaken voluntarily, but rather from an irresistible compulsion. Much to be pitied are those unfortunate ones who are crammed together into a bus, casting desperate glances toward the grazing cows which are granted the privilege of staying in one place or of leisurely placing one leg in front of the other, while the passengers' lot is to continue onward toward the next pass.

And swerving between the drivers on four wheels are those on two wheels, unrecognisable in their black leather garb. The locals claim they are so tightly packed and cushioned in leather that after a fall, they can even walk with a

broken foot. They are damned to death-defying manoeu-
vres such as passing at full speed on a blind curve, forcing
the overtaken vehicle to brake suddenly. Wherever they go,
they spread fear and terror. They mostly travel together in
darkly-clad convoys, often with a woman perched behind
the driver, hanging on to him in lust and apprehension with
black arms. When they call out to one another in harsh
voices, it is the only noise heard above the deep, deafening
drone of the pass procession.

The least fortunate, however, puff their way up the
mountain with bent backs on light-weight steel bicycles.
They try to make light of the agony of their ascent by wearing colourful cycling gear, but as they stagger from their
saddles with twisted mouths to fill up their Isostar bottles
at the Tschamut fountain, it becomes clear that they are not
up here because they want to be, but because they have to
be. Even when they're whizzing down the mountain, passing cars and even skilfully overtaking buses, one hears no
shouts of jubilation. Instead their stern expressions hint at
the secret power lurking behind their handlebars.

There's no standing around. Don't be fooled by those
who are having a picnic on trampled grass at a place in the
road broad enough for cars to overtake. They sit on folding
chairs and slurp drinks from their thermos bottles, but their
eyes are not on the beauties of nature but fixed on the traffic, on their fellow sufferers who can't escape the destiny
of the street. Even the rest area on the pass summit is
marked by restlessness. Meals and big ice cream coupes

are still served on the terraces of restaurants, but more often "gottapay" is murmured, and the conversations of the stocky men in blue undershirts sweating heavily and wolfing down their sausages aren't free and easy in a Sunday mood, but keep circling morbidly around the vehicle of their damnation. The women sit heavily and listlessly next to them, writing postcards to those left behind.

It's only when the sun starts to set that the commotion gradually disappears. The last saddlebag biker realizes from his map clamped on his handlebars that he won't be able to reach the summit today and seeks refuge in the dormitory of the 'Rheinquelle'. Some motorists shine their headlights in the direction of the lowland, and the lead and sulphur cloud hovering over the whole procession dissolves and the air becomes crystal clear. A profound silence descends once again on the Oberalp where nothing can be heard but the majestic droning of the hay-drying machines and the sudden hush of the mountain streams, as, one after the other, they are swallowed up by being tunnelled into the water system of the Curnera valley. ₒₒₒ

The Caravan

I had never looked so deep into the milk jug as this time when I wanted to clean it so thoroughly that the white rings near the bottom would disappear. Therefore I had never noticed that at the bottom of the jug, a sandy desert was spreading out that I could view as if from an airplane.

Between the many dunes that resembled a stiffened body of water, I suddenly noticed there was a caravan moving forward slowly. I flew down lower and saw that it must be a caravan of camels. The animals' long necks could be seen clearly moving back and forth in the slow elastic rhythm of their gait.

Two camel-driving figures walked along with them, one in front and the other at the back of the caravan, wearing long white robes flapping in the wind that seemed quite strong in spite of the light blue weather. Just as I was going to take a closer look at what the camels were carrying, I heard how the camel driver at the back called out something sounding highly agitated to the one at the front.

Both of them threw themselves to the ground and at the same moment, a herd of elephants attacked the camel caravan from behind, trampled them down, and each elephant hastily gobbled down a camel. Then the elephants trotted away leisurely. The camel drivers raised their heads and found themselves alone in the desert with the ivory carvings that had fallen from the bolts of fabric torn to tatters in the sand.

I lifted my head from the milk jug, looked inside again, but the desert had disappeared.

I knew it was impossible that something like that could take place at the bottom of a milk jug.

Nevertheless, that's what I saw. ∘∘∘

The Gateau

When you walk from the station in Locarno down to the old part of the town, after a short distance you pass an arcade where young people dressed in colourful caps and T-shirts are sitting in front of carton plates of chips and glasses of Coca-Cola. The metal tables and chairs spread out on different levels are not entirely appropriate for the fastfood scene. If you look more carefully, you see why. These are the steps leading up to the garden of the Grand Hotel Locarno, which is there in the background like a dream from a different age. It is surrounded by cypresses, palms and luxuriant rhododendron bushes. There with its extensive central terrace, amidst pillars bearing bowls of flowers, are figures solidified into stone, as if at that moment the dance music of a spa orchestra had just come to an end.

Do you want to go on to the Piazza Grande or do you have a moment to hear a story that began in this hotel?

I heard it in a building of the same period and not really dissimilar in appearance to the Grand Hotel, an old people's home in one of the valleys behind Locarno. The building was somewhat more modest, its central wing set back behind two corner towers with a large cobblestoned square in front, leading into a pergola of gloxinia. In Locarno the name of the hotel was emblazoned in interchangeable, illuminated letters, but here the name of the benefactor was written permanently on the old people's home in a mosaic lettering.

Last year a private matter took me to this nursing home. The canton of Ticino had begun to simplify the organisation of numerous plots of land and to recommend that owners combine or exchange them. Having a small piece of land with a barn on an Alpine pasture where we like to spend a few days in summer, I received a similar request and decided to go see the owner of the neighbouring plot of land. He had recently come to live in this old people's home. We knew one another and he was pleased about my visit. He complained about his declining eyesight, his diabetes which was affecting his legs so that he could hardly walk any more, and the decline of his whole body summed up in one word: aging. He agreed at once to the exchange of land I suggested to him, asked about the condition of the spring, the stream and the old chestnut trees, and told me about his childhood days when there were still six hundred head of cattle in the village, of which not a single cow remains today.

While we were speaking, the man with whom he shared a room lay motionless in bed, his mouth half open, giving from time to time a gentle groan. When I asked him how he was, he did not react.

"He can't hear," said my acquaintance, "he'll soon be a hundred, and I think he has wanted to die for some time, but he can't."

We continued our conversation and I asked if there had once been wild boar up there on the slopes. At this the man in the next bed raised his head and said "Un giorno vanno trovare la torta." "One day they will find the gateau," and then his head sank back again.

My acquaintance smiled and said that was the only thing the poor fellow still said, and for that reason they always called him 'la torta', a nickname which he had brought with him to the home and which he had clearly had in his village all his life. But nobody knew what the reason for it was, and there were no family visitors one could ask.

I stepped over to the old man's bed, bent over him and asked: "Dove vanno trovare la torta?" "Where will they find the gateau?"

Without opening his eyes, he said, "Nel lago." "In the lake."

I asked my acquaintance whether he had read that recently the Lake Maggiore police were searching for someone who had drowned in the lake and had found a large tin box with the inscription 'Grand Hotel Locarno'. In it were rusty detonators that could have belonged to a cargo of dynamite. All this had given rise to some speculation.

I had hardly said this when the old man sat up in bed, opened his eyes wide and shouted: "L' hanno finalmente trovata!" "They have found it at last!"

"The gateau?" I asked and added: "But there was dynamite in it."

Then the caregiver appeared with lunch and was quite

astonished to see the old man sitting up in bed. She was even more surprised when he told me in a clear voice that I should go now and return in the afternoon, when he would tell me the story of the gateau.

I went to an inn where they served a wonderful polenta with leg of rabbit and when I visited the home again in the afternoon, the old man had undergone a strange transformation. He was sitting in the armchair by the window and was wearing a blue jacket with braids on the front and a cap with the inscription 'Grand Hotel Locarno'. He sat there in such a way that you might have requested him immediately to bring a case up to your room. I could hardly believe that the same man, who had been breathing with such difficulty when I had seen him in the morning, was now telling this story without hesitation.

"Sit down," he said and pointed to the chair reserved for visitors. "Although I don't know you, I want to tell you my story because you brought me news about the discovery of the tin box. I have already spoken to Righetti about it," he said, nodding towards his room mate who suffered from diabetes. "He wants to listen too."

My name is Ernesto Tonini and I was born in this valley in 1904. You are a German-speaking Swiss, aren't you? I don't know whether you have any idea of how we lived at that time. It was simply a battle for survival which we waged from the valley bottom to the edge of the forest. Every square metre that could be cultivated was valuable. Every chestnut tree amounted to so many meals for hungry stomachs. Children often had to go to the upland pastures with the goats and sheep for the whole summer and their sole sustenance was three or four litres of goat's milk per day. Every family had too many children, and if the mother died bearing her seventh child or the father was bitten by an adder when mowing and no antidote was available, the children were given to relatives. Here they usually toiled away from cockcrow till past sunset, or they were sent to the orphanage.

I was lucky and got sent to the orphanage and then, when I left school, I was fortunate again and got a job as an errand boy in the Grand Hotel Locarno.

Of course they tried to get the most out of us. Duties began at 5 a.m. when we had to sweep the large terrace and the front square. We had to fetch the rolls from the bakers, and you were a poor soul if you were caught having eaten one. The head cook counted them and deducted it from your wages, if that is what you could call 50 Rappen a day. A roll cost 10 Rappen.

I do not want to bore you further with what we had to endure, but just add that being the youngest meant everything the older ones tried to avoid was thrust onto you.

We lived four to a room with two bunk beds with just enough room for one person to stand between them. To the others, who all came from Locarno, Ascona or Tenero, I was the fool from the valley. I had no opportunity to see my brothers and sisters. To be brief, I was lonely, miserable and poor, and surrounded every day by people who were sociable, cheerful and rich. And so it was that I became a communist."

Ernesto Tonini smiled and looked at us in turn. We must have had rather surprised expressions on our faces.

"You would never have thought it, would you?"

We both shook our heads and he went on:

"The baker's boy, who handed me the bread each day, took me on one of my few free evenings to a meeting that was held in a printing works in Muralto. I called it a meeting but it was more like a conspiracy — six or seven men were there and sometimes Giuletta too, the printer's daughter. The printer spoke about the plans Marx had for a world in which there were no longer rich and poor, but everything belonged to everybody, and he said that our great comrade Lenin had travelled from Switzerland to Russia and had overthrown the Tsar to bring about such a world. He told us that for the time being, it was better for us not to say anything about this where we worked because the rich ruled here and we would be thrown out immediately, for instance, from the Grand Hotel Locarno.

I went along with this, but from the moment I joined the communists, the world looked quite different to me. I was more at ease and did a better job because now I knew that things would not stay like this. One day I would be able to invite my brothers and sisters, who were working as farmhands or in the quarries or who were still in the orphanage, into the rooms at the Grand Hotel with a view of the lake.

Because I looked quite smart I got a tip from time to time, and I bought myself some small text books to learn German, English and French. I kept them in my pocket and took them out during my errands to familiarise myself with these languages. The printer kept on telling us that we all belonged to a cell and that it was quite possible that one of us could even be sent abroad where world history was being made.

When I carried the cases belonging to foreign guests up to their rooms, I always tried to say something in their language and to learn from them. This made me popular, and the guests often asked for little Ernesto to go with them to the station or bring tea up to their room. This did not go unnoticed in the hotel, and three years later I was assigned to room service. I was even employed from time to time as an auxiliary waiter. And on two evenings in the month at our meetings, I heard how comrade Lenin was shaking Russia up and that the workers and soldiers' councils of the revolutionary Räterepublik had failed in Munich and that this should be a warning to us about how difficult it is to carry out a revolution here.

And then suddenly world history came to Locarno. In the autumn of 1925 the Prime Ministers of half Europe gathered here, in the Ticino of all places, to discuss the consequences of the First World War. As far as I understood it, the main purpose was to restore Germany as a normal member of Europe. We noted that this was not yet the case, as far as Germany was concerned, because all delegations, apart from the German one, were accommodated here in the Grand Hotel. The English, the French, the Italians, the Belgians and, wait a minute, the Czechs were there too. Mr. Benesch and his wife, who always wore a straw hat, came a little later, and then the Poles.

The whole of Locarno went wild during those two weeks. Between two and three hundred journalists raced each day to the Palazzo di Giustizia where the meetings were held and where they were not allowed in, and then to the Grand Hotel to the press conferences, where they gained no information either. Then they went to the association of banks where they could telephone and send telegrams. Politicians whose names were only known from the newspapers were suddenly to be seen in the flesh. Stresemann, the German with his shining bald head, drank beer in the evenings on the Piazza Grande. The Frenchman, Briand, short and a little hunched, went on one occasion to the cinema. You saw Chamberlain walking on the beach with his wife. Of course, they were there quite close to us in the Grand Hotel at the breakfast table or at dinner, and the staff slaved away from early in the morning till late at night and nobody had time off. Once when I was dog-tired and wanted to go to my room, the head cook intercepted me shortly before twelve on the backstairs. I had to help him butter some rolls, which I then had to take to a midnight press conference. There I learnt how Grandi, Mussolini's right-hand man, was threatening all Italian journalists that if a single word of the draft treaty appeared in one of their newspapers, the newspaper would be banned at once. And then I was allowed to serve my rolls while Luigi, a second auxiliary waiter, filled their glasses with champagne. So I learnt what freedom of the press meant and it became clear why the printer spoke of the fascists with indignation.

It was not only Locarno that was in uproar, but our little cell too. The communists, our printer taught us, were strictly against these negotiations. A Germany that was functioning again would strengthen the right-wing bourgeois forces in Europe, and this would make the revolutionary uprising more difficult. The communists were therefore of the opinion that this conference had to be sabotaged.

I learnt how seriously they took the matter when the printer kept me back after our meeting shortly before the conference began. He told me that, as I was working in the Grand Hotel, I would come closest to the politicians without arousing any suspicion and that all the comrades were expecting me to do something great for the world revolution. "What kind of thing do you mean?" I asked and he opened a briefcase containing a few sticks of dynamite and showed me how to ignite the fuse. "It is set at ten seconds", he said, "Then nobody will have time to escape."

I went pale. "That means –"

"Yes, Ernesto, that means that your name will be in all the history books. The Piazza Grande will be called Piazza Ernesto Tonini. Do you understand?"

"Yes, boss."

"Workers of the world"—

"— unite," I murmured and set off home with the briefcase under my arm and, because the single room I had at the time was as large as a better broom closet, I just stowed it in my suitcase which I kept under the bed.

I had reached my decision quickly. Until now my life had been hard and joyless; I had hardly any friends outside the cell. I could foresee little chance of promotion in the hotel trade. Nobody would miss me. But my name would go round the world and later my brothers and sisters would be able to drink lemonade in a square bearing their brother's name."

Ernesto Tonini paused and asked me if I could pass him the cup of tea from the bedside table, and when he had it in his hand he drank it in a few mouthfuls and ran his tongue over his dry lips. I poured him a second cup from the tea pot, but he declined and continued his story.

"The conference began and the question was where could I hit as many participants as possible at one time. Apart from checking that the chandelier hanging four floors above the entrance hall was secure, one of the few security measures in the hotel was that the delegations should sit as far as possible from one another at dinner. Therefore, I had to consider which of the delegations I wished to assassinate. The most important ones in my vicinity were without doubt the English and the French. I had already decided on the English delegation because Chamberlain was the conference chairman and because Madame

Briand had given me a tip when I brought a bouquet of flowers from Sindaco up to her room.

Chance was offering me an opportunity that history had to envy.

One of the most important guests to frequent our hotel, causing everybody to stand to attention in his presence, was a Frenchman called Loucheur. He was a textbook capitalist and the printer uttered his name with hatred whenever he spoke of the starvation wages of the steamship company and the Centovalli railway, both of which belonged to Monsieur Loucheur. It was also rumoured that it was really thanks to him that the conference had actually been held in Locarno. Now Monsieur Loucheur ordered a large gateau from the pastry chef in the hotel. At midday on the following day it had to be brought to his motor ship, 'Fior d'arancia'. It soon leaked out that the top men at the conference were to be invited for an excursion so that they could talk amongst themselves in a more pleasant atmosphere.

The gateau was a rich speciality of the Ticino, served with Merlot and green Veltliner wines. It was to be ready on the table for twelve people, and later during the trip this large gateau would be served with coffee. To my great surprise, I was chosen to bring the gateau to the ship and help the head waiter serve.

One reason for this was a large banquet in the evening. Its preparation required the mobilisation of all available staff. Probably another significant factor was that I could make myself understood to some extent in German, English and French.

You can imagine that I slept little that night, and perhaps you can also imagine how I brought the dynamite onto the ship the next day. The gateau had two tiers and the pastry chef had written on it in cream 'Pace' and 'Locarno'. It was placed in a large tin box closed with fasteners. When I carried it out of the kitchen, I first went into my room, opened it and shoved the sticks of dynamite into the cake until only the fuse was still visible. Then I fastened the box again and carried it like a small monstrance the short distance to the mooring where the head waiter was already waiting for me. As space was very tight in the ship's small saloon, he had designated a place for the gateau under a seat on the rear deck. This also had the advantage of keeping it cooler; after all, it was still mid October. So I stowed it there and then listened with half an ear to his instructions for serving. The most important thing was that I could feel the matches in my pocket. I was ready. World history could unfold.

In the meantime, the ministers and secretaries of state, who suspected nothing, were following one another onto the ship that would lead them to their death. Chamberlain, Briand, Stresemann, Luther, Sciaiola and the rest of them were being welcomed by Monsieur Loucheur. Then, when the ship cast off travelling in the direction of Luino and they were reaching for their sandwiches, the neck of salted pork and slices of salami, raising their glasses of wine and repeating the words 'League of Nations', something curious happened.

You will understand that I was rather nervous about what lay ahead, and so it was that I spilt some white wine on the dress of Lady Chamberlain of all people, the only lady on board.

This brought an angry glance from the head waiter. Lady Chamberlain looked at me with consideration and asked: "Are you in love, young man?"

It was suddenly clear to me that I was really in love and that I was in love with Giulietta, the daughter of the printer, whom I liked to admire when she brought us conspirators something to drink before she left again. I realised that I had been waiting some time for the opportunity to see her alone, to invite her to go for a walk with me, that I was not just toying with this idea but I was dying to kiss her and embrace her and that I had no desire whatever to go down in history before I had gone out with this girl. To my great astonishment I heard myself replying: "Yes I am, Madame, and I beg your pardon."

Ernesto Tonini grasped the curved armrest, pulled his feeble body forward as far as he could, gave us a piercing look, and went on: "And when the moment came for the head waiter to tell me to fetch the gateau, I went onto the rear deck and could do nothing other than intentionally trip over a bench, dropping the tin box with the 'Pace and Locarno' gateau over the railing into the lake where it slowly sank.

The head waiter's indignation knew no bounds and Monsieur Loucheur hissed 'connard' and 'cretin', and I probably would have had a thrashing on the spot had it not been for Lady Chamberlain. She placed her hand on mine and said in a conciliatory tone: "He is in love, gentlemen — why don't you love each other too?"

I have never turned as red as I was on that occasion, and who knows whether Germany would have been accepted into the League of Nations without Lady Chamberlain's advocacy of love, and so perhaps I did in fact have some influence on the course of the world. Naturally the story immediately went around. All my colleagues always called me 'la torta' from that moment on. And if Lady Chamberlain had not put in a word for me with the hotel management, I would definitely have been fired.

Nobody has ever discovered what was in the gateau, but the next day I went to the printer and told him that his sticks of dynamite were lying in a tin box at the bottom of Lake Maggiore, and that it would be better if he carried out the next assassination himself instead of leaving it to a nitwit like me. I added that I would not be coming to his meetings anymore and that I no longer believed in communism if it entailed killing such nice people as Mr. and Lady Chamberlain and even killing myself in the process.

However, I gave him my word that I would never tell anybody about it and he was very grateful for that. Furthermore, he later became my father-in-law because Giulietta liked me. We kissed and embraced in the short time we were a couple. She died young and childless of tuberculosis and I still love her even today. I love her and Lady Chamberlain, who both prevented me from taking a place in world history."

The old man sank back exhausted into the armchair and for a while the room was absolutely quiet. Then he asked me to fetch the two tooth-mugs from the washstand, to rinse them out and to open the bottom part of his cupboard. There, behind his small case, in which he must have once stored the dynamite, was a bottle of Grappa and a pewter goblet with the inscription 'Grand Hotel Locarno'.

Although he was trembling, he insisted on pouring us some himself, which he did without spilling a drop. While it was starting to rain outside and darkness was gradually falling, we drank the whole bottle, slowly, in small sips.

When I phoned my acquaintance two days later to tell him our exchange had been accepted by the Land Registry Office, he told me that Ernesto Tonini had died peacefully in the night. ooo

Discount Offer

Fish, meat pies, pre-packaged sauces, sausage meat-balls, noodles — I take these items one after the other out of the box-like compartment where they have been transported by the conveyor belt after being scanned and I put them in my bag. The lady cashier asks each customer if they wish to benefit from the following discount offer: shop for at least 35 Swiss francs, eight times until the end of the month, and we'll stamp your card. The ninth time you'll get 10% off your purchase.

If a customer decides to take the card, the cashier stamps it cheerfully saying: "You see, here's your first stamp!" I also take one home although I am sure that I will never use it.

The reaction of the next customer behind me is quite different though. She is a small wrinkled woman wearing a thick black coat who answers by putting on the counter a small bundle of those coupons that are posted to you together with a voucher of 5 Swiss francs for the Cumulus loyalty card. Printed on these vouchers are promisingly large amounts that can be used only when making a specific purchase, such as 50 Swiss francs when buying a complete set of percussion drills or 125 Swiss francs when purchasing a garden swing, for instance.

The cashier explains to the elderly lady that she can

use the coupons only in a particular branch and only when buying the items indicated on the vouchers, then she pushes them back again. The elderly woman stares at the vouchers for a second before pushing them back determinedly to the shop assistant who repeats the explanation she has already given. But all to no avail. Her friendliness makes no impression on this little old woman in the thick black coat who apparently doesn't speak any of the languages spoken here – who knows which foreign tongue she's familiar with, maybe Kurdish, Georgian or Kazakh. But she can read the numbers and they seem to promise her that she will get something, so she pushes all the vouchers over the small depression on the counter for the change back to the cashier and looks at her piercingly. She's in the Promised Land here, isn't she? No, she isn't. The shop assistant repeats her explanation, a bit louder and more slowly this time, takes the Cumulus loyalty card from the bundle of vouchers, runs it over the scanner which acknowledges it with a bleep, and hands it back to the customer again who, without comprehending or complaining, puts it finally back into her purse together with the empty promises. These numbers, as she has suspected all along, have just lied and deceived her. They are for others, just like everything else here, for others but not for her whose eyes are used to seeing the steppes or the infinite highlands that lie far beyond the cash register and the shop assistant and this shopping centre where one doesn't want to let her participate in the riches available here which she is entitled to after a life full of privation. ₒₒₒ

Accidents

The street where I live is very quiet. It's a residential street with hardly any traffic. In spite of this, people who live here have surprisingly many accidents.

The butcher with the little moustache, for example, who lives in the house diagonally opposite ours, is missing his left index finger.

The woman who works at the post office and lives in the new building on the corner is missing three fingers of her right hand. I am always amazed how quickly she flips through the piles of payment slips.

In winter a teacher slipped on the unsalted school yard and still suffers from the fracture in her upper arm. Now it's summer and I keep asking myself how anyone can break their upper arm in a fall.

A young boy broke his forearm when jumping off a low wall. That's easier to understand since this young boy is my son. All of his buddies have signed his cast.

The carpenter next door is missing the tip of one finger. It was bitten off by his dog.

Further down the street a man burned his right hand when he tried to light a pile of wet branches with petrol. Each of his fingers is bandaged individually.

An assistant pastor hides a black swollen eye under

his sunglasses. He got it at the indoor swimming pool from a swimmer doing the crawl.

A man in charge of screening luggage lost his eye from a metal band that flew into his face when he used pincers to open a bunch of briquettes.

An engineer on his racing bike was hit by a delivery truck and had to spend seven months in hospital. Now he goes to the market again on Saturdays, but something is wrong with the way he walks.

Lots of people walk with a crutch, some even with two of them. And sometimes on nice days when everybody is outside, I have the feeling that each one is dragging a stiff leg and there is hardly anybody who can really walk properly upright and unencumbered. Yes, actually we are all injured as if we were in the middle of a war. ₒₒₒ

The Execution

Yesterday I witnessed an execution. The woman sentenced to death was about fifty years old. She approached the place of execution in a car from the right, overtaking three stationary vehicles waiting at a stop sign and went towards the gap in the traffic which they had made for her. As she approached this space a sports coupé came at full speed from the opposite direction, obscured from her view by the queue of oncoming traffic. It was driven by the executioner who was running late.

At the very moment the condemned's car squeezed through the gap, the executioner's coupé ploughed into it from the right causing it to momentarily leave the ground before it came to a standstill to the left of the crossroads.

The condemned was slumped unconscious against the window with blood trickling down her forehead. As the blue-uniformed executioner's guards opened the door to move her body, she was still breathing but her short breaths were increasingly mixed with a choking cough.

The executioner didn't look much like the harbinger of death as he got out of his car. Looking helplessly on as water trickled from his cracked radiator, his whole body shook and he gave the overall impression of a man filled with despair.

Later it transpired that he was unaware that he had been appointed the local executioner. Similarly the woman had, according to her family, never been informed that she had been sentenced to death and as for me, well, nobody told me that I was to be called as a witness. ooo

Destination Selzach

The queue moves forward one step.

It's the turn of the man in front of me, a big, broad-shouldered man from the Far East — an Indian, I suppose.

He names his destination: "Selzach."

The woman behind the window of the ticket counter frowns, and over the window's loudspeaker she says: "Pardon?"

The Indian repeats the place name: "Selzach."

The woman raises her eyebrows: "Seuzach?" she asks and nods, trying to be helpful.

The Indian replies: "No, Selzach." He pronounces it as clearly as possible.

The woman shakes her head. This place – she has never heard of it. The man must be mistaken. "Doesn't exist," she says.

The Indian sees that she doesn't understand him and tries to explain: "Two after Solothurn."

As the woman in the ticket office puts a piece of paper on the turnplate for him to write down his out-of-the-world destination, I call out to her: "Of course Selzach exists!" and add: "I am from Solothurn and should know." I visualise the map of the canton of Solothurn in front of me with the places circled in red that we had to learn by heart in 5th grade. On this map Selzach is between the towns of Solothurn and Grenchen, and that's where it still is, two stations from Solothurn, as the Indian man remarked correctly. But now the piece of paper has already been pushed in front of the railway ticket woman, and she types into her computer what he has written down: "Selzeg," and then she tells him there is no such place as Selzeg, only Selzach, as she has found out in the meantime. She asks him if he wants a single.

But the Indian wants a return, back to Zurich. He pays for his ticket which is printed using a program that the Swiss Railway Company purchased from a software firm in India.

Then he walks away from the ticket counter and ends an act for three people where each of them was right, yet nobody was satisfied. ooo

The Motorway Mystery

Are we more sensitive when we are sitting in a car?

At first glance the opposite seems to be the case. We hear about road rowdies. Police chiefs arrange press conferences documenting and deploring all the wild driving on roads. The fewer the chances are to overtake, the more people start overtaking like lunatics. Impatience makes them ruthless, insensitive to the dangers. Nobody getting in his car in the morning believes that in the evening he will have to be rescued by being sawed out of a metal rubble heap. Nobody can imagine the bang of a child bouncing off the bonnet of the automobile and the force with which it will be whirled into the air and hurtled to the ground. Nobody can imagine it, and nobody wants to imagine it. When you experience it, it's already too late. Driving cars is numbing.

And yet a car is an interior space capable of producing the most wondrous of moods. Or haven't you ever experienced how well you can talk to someone when you are returning home as a twosome from somewhere? There's darkness all around you, from time to time headlights like glowing fish coming towards you and disappearing again, and the regular hum of the motor. You don't have to look into each other's eyes when you talk like in a train where you sit unrelentingly across from each other. But you stare in two parallel lines that never cross, not even infinitely.

And yet it's all close enough to touch. And suddenly there is an atmosphere that is so human and intimate, an atmosphere for confessions, for revelations, for sudden intuitions. And also when one is driving alone, something similar can occur — the combination of movement and monotony on a long trip can awaken uncommon feelings, a thirst for adventure, a hunger for spring, the secret willingness to experience the improbable.

How else can it be explained that since the existence of cars there have been stories about weird hitchhikers? For a long time well known in the whole region of the Alps there was the one about the woman in black. She stood with her hand raised in black clothes at the curve of a mountain road. If you gave her a ride, she sat in the rear seat of the car saying nothing, and when you turned around to her after a while, she had disappeared. It was worse when you saw her at the side of the road and drove on thinking you wouldn't pick her up, only to discover a short time later that she was sitting in the back seat anyway.

Recently a woman in white appeared in the Belchen tunnel that goes south from Basel under the Jura mountains. Many people had seen her or claimed to have seen her. The story got around of her getting into the car and of her sudden disappearance. The police were reluctant to give explanations. They merely stated that no patrol car had ever come across such a figure.

Together with the woman in white, there was also a profusion of men coming out of God only knows which cracks in our mountainous country, or out of our anxious souls. These men were spread out over the roads of Switzerland and raised their hands to stop cars. These were different types of men, some old and shabby, others with clothes from the previous century, still others who were elegant and with white hair and a black briefcase. It wasn't enough for them to get in your car and say nothing, but they wove in comments and made prophesies. These were simple things admittedly. But for most folks they were bloodcurdling because afterwards the passenger disappeared, right out of the back seat.

It's beside the point whether such things actually happened or whether the parties involved only imagined them. There is an effect in any case, and if it is not true, it is at least effective. This is why from the very beginning I had no doubts that there must be some truth to the rumours about the accidents at Kestenholz.

These accidents were the worst and at the same time the most unaccountable in the country. They all occurred on the longest straight stretch of our network of motorways, shortly after Egerkingen up on the hill of Kestenholz. Nothing there disturbs the view and the road is open — no bridge, no road sign, no exit. You can drive through the lowlands at the foot of the Jura mountains with a downright Californian feeling of serenity and broadmindedness, out into the wide world, at least until you get to Oensingen.

Why then, did it keep happening precisely there,

again and again, that motorists in the overtaking lane would suddenly swerve out of this lane either back into the right lane or into the crash barrier in the middle of the motorway? This manoeuvre was always fatal for the driver, and not only for him alone as usually there was a vehicle in the right lane and a horrible collision when the passing car attempted to get back in the right lane. And when it swerved to the left into the steel cables of the crash barriers, which are normally too weak to prevent the car from crossing to the oncoming lanes, it met oncoming traffic, causing a frontal collision.

Since no driver of any of the crashed cars survived such an accident, you always had to try to get a picture of what happened from the observations of the others involved. But there was never anything that motorists noticed to explain such a panicked reaction.

Birds of prey diving down suddenly to catch their prey are known to be the cause of similar accidents but nobody had ever seen one there. Not a single witness was found either for rabbits or other small animals that might have hopped into the roadway. A truck driver explained it best who had just been passed by an unlucky driver who had just veered to the left and rolled over to the other side of the road. The truck driver summarized what he might possibly have seen in the other lane: "Nothing, really absolutely nothing."

But it could not be absolutely nothing that in the middle of the day, usually even in good weather, impelled drivers to make such a disastrous change of direction. And so all sorts of speculations were put forth.

Earth-ray devotees were convinced their time had come and positioned themselves with pendulums in the emergency lanes. Water diviners showed up and requested that they be allowed to walk around on the overtaking lane to check it. Magnetic field enthusiasts explained their wave-bundling theories. Astrophilosophers spoke about a temporary focus of intensive cosmic rays. Proposed solutions to the problem ranged from wrapping the crash barrier ropes with copper wiring to putting a roof over the whole section of the road, or sticking metal plates from the edge of the motorway up to the Dünnern, the little stream that flows along the stretch of the road.

The police were at a loss and did nothing. But when a sports car, trying to pass a semitrailor truck, drove under the truck's wheels and was dragged along and smashed, a sign was put up at this spot limiting the allowed speed to 100 km. Anyone who knows how difficult it is in this country to get authorities to introduce speed limits will realize that the danger was taken seriously.

But where the danger came from was still not clear. At times one heard comments from people living in the area, especially from the elderly, that they shouldn't have been allowed to remove the boundary stone of the rye farmer. This referred to an old story previously told in the region about a farmer who, after his death, appeared in the nighttime to lug the moved boundary stone back to its original place. A woman who collects myths brought this to the attention of the police.

The official who was given the job of collecting evidence gave a sigh as he put the piece of paper with this note on the pile of letters about the intensive cosmic rays and the metal plates. He only thought about it again when the next accident occurred.

This was now the first accident where there was a survivor in the vehicle in the overtaking lane. The bus of a wedding party wanted to pass the bus of another wedding party when it suddenly braked so hard that the furniture transport truck in the lane behind it crashed into it. It was thrown across the lane and was also hit by several other cars in the right lane which were all wedged into one another. It was the biggest accident that had ever taken place at this spot. More than a dozen people were killed and there were many who were seriously injured. An official day of mourning was declared like for an airplane crash.

The bus driver was one of those who died, and also the passengers right behind him. But the two children who sat in the front seat next to the bus driver were by some lucky coincidence not injured and could be questioned about the course of events.

What they testified gave the examining magistrate goose bumps down his back. Their descriptions matched, and they testified without the slightest doubt that suddenly there was a huge wagon in front of them — a hay wagon drawn by two horses — and at the front of the wagon there was a man standing and swinging his whip while looking back and laughing. The bus driver immediately slammed on the brakes, and they were conscious again only when they were being pulled out of the bus.

As this became known, the myth collector, an elderly teacher with a vivid gaze, went again to the police and requested permission also to ask the children questions in the presence of the examining magistrate. The head of police asked her if she believed the story of these young children. Absolutely, she said, reminding them that she had brought this possibility to their attention a year ago. The head of police arranged an appointment with the woman and the two children where the examining magistrate would also be present.

The woman who collects myths found just the right tone to speak to the children — two brothers, one nine and the other seven years old. She let them tell their whole story again and when she cautiously enquired if there was actually anything on the hay wagon, the older boy said the hay wagon was empty and he had mostly looked at the man with the crazy look in his eyes. The younger boy didn't say anything but when the teacher asked him again, he said yes, he had looked at the wagon and saw that lying on it was a stone. What kind of a stone? It was like a grave stone, the younger boy said. The teacher pulled out a photo and showed it to the boys: "Was it this one?" "Yes," the boy answered, "it was that one." It was a photograph of an old boundary stone with a hole in its upper left corner.

She suspected right away, said the myth collector, that the rye farmer was back again, but now she knew it for sure. This spooky figure from the last century kept appearing until the stone was returned to its correct position on the border between the Dünneren stream acre and the Kestenholz field. After that, he didn't come anymore. They had to move the boundary stone when constructing the motorway. The Historical Museum in Olten was interested in it and it can be seen there. Where precisely the boundary stone had stood she would have to leave to the engineers, but she was convinced that since the opening of the motorway, the rye farmer had been trying to get the stone back to its former position and that all the car crashes were caused by their drivers' efforts to avoid crashing into it.

The head of police was a bit embarrassed. "We'll check it out," he finally said and gave the Surveyers Office instructions to localize precisely where the stone had formerly stood.

It turned out that the stone was formerly positioned precisely under the present passing lane in the direction of Berne where the land registry shows the border between the Dünneren stream acre and the Kestenholz field.

The head of police called a meeting of higher officials and also had the woman who collects myths attend.

"If your assumption is correct," the head of police said, "and the cars really crashed in attempting to avoid colliding with this appearance of the hay wagon, then we have to assume there will be more accidents."

"That's for sure," said the teacher.

"Do you see a way this could possibly be averted?" asked the head of police.

"Yes," the teacher said, "the rye farmer has to be redeemed."

This made everyone uncomfortable. The head of police made nervous coughing noises.

"And just how can we make him redeemed?" he asked, obviously disgusted by this expression.

The woman who collects myths smiled.

"By putting the stone back again where it belongs."

Everyone present knew that was coming but they started groaning anyway.

"Impossible! That's insane!" yelled a federal official from Berne who was in charge of road traffic. "Reconstruct the motorway because of an old boundary stone! What century are we living in anyway?"

"But if we . . ." the head of police tried to say, "but if we put the stone back as close as possible in the middle strip between the dual motorway just three, four metres from the former position? Do you think that would be any help?"

"Hardly," replied the myth collector. "Ghosts are rather pedantic."

This ended the meeting.

Then the question was brought to the cantonal government and to the federal authorities, and they came to a realistic decision: That is to say, considering the technical advances of today, one should not resort to hasty measures, not on the evidence of spooky stories that are told by children. And therefore, a reduction of the speed limit to 100 km was the only justifiable measure to be taken and, in addition, drivers were recommended to be especially careful on this stretch of the road.

Only half a year later — when a bus taking people from a nursing home on an excursion rolled over during an abrupt swerving manoeuvre and burst into flames — was the passing lane closed for good, and the stone was placed at its former spot.

Since then no further accidents have occurred. It has not yet been decided if a right lane will be constructed again, but it is unlikely considering the current financial situation. So this nuisance will have to be put up with. And of course, like every bottleneck, there are constantly traffic hold-ups. Many motorists, when seeing the stone while passing this narrowing of the road marked as a construction site, shake their heads ranting about the government. Others, like me for instance, when seeing this stone feel an enormous, almost indescribable satisfaction. ₀₀₀

The Daily Death

My grandmother told me once what she thought as a young girl of the death of Jesus Christ. To hang a few hours on the cross — that's nothing, she thought. I have to go to the factory every day.

In the early years of the 20th century, a day's work at the factory lasted 11 hours, from 6 am to noon, and from 1 to 6 pm. On Saturdays workers stopped working one hour earlier so that they could make preparations for Sunday. On Sundays they had to go to church to hear about the death of Jesus. My grandmother lived in Sisseln and had to go on foot to church in Eiken, the neighbouring village. The names of young people who missed going to church were called out from the pulpit. My grandmother went to church most Sundays, but one of her younger brothers never went and his name was called out every Sunday. The father of my grandmother, my great-grandfather, never went to church, but sent his children to church just like he sent them to work in the factory.

The factory was located in Säckingen on the German side of the Rhine. It was a weaving mill. When a thread broke, the machines had to be stopped so that the thread could either be tied and threaded again into the machine or replaced completely. The time when the machines were not running was deducted from the workers' wages. My grand-mother wrote a letter to the director of the factory com-plaining about this — the factory workers were not to blame when he gave them poor thread that was constantly breaking. As she secretly hoped, because of this letter she was almost thrown out of the factory. Her behaviour, the director said, reminded him of the way members of the so-cialist youth organisation act in Zurich. And if she weren't such a good worker, he would fire her immediately. From that time on, however, the thread was of better quality.

My grandmother also met my grandfather at the fac-tory. He came every day on foot from Zuzgen, one and one-half hours' walk in the morning and one and one-half hours again in the evening. My grandfather told me that during this long journey he made together with three others, they would often sing songs.

He and my grandmother got married when they were young and I am their descendant. ooo

The Contrabass Player

It sometimes happens that an uninvited guest appears at a party intended only for invited guests, and I'd like to tell you about such a party.

A woman, a bookkeeper in a city council office, celebrated her fiftieth birthday together with her partner. At the small restaurant they had booked for the party, they had lunch with about forty invited guests. As the restaurant didn't have any big dining-rooms, it was closed to other guests that Sunday, and the main entrance was locked.

The woman had been married before for many years to a man who had been a well-known and popular contrabass player in his spare time, and who one morning was found dead in bed without warning. When organising her party, the woman had asked a former colleague and friend of her former husband's to play some music between the courses and after the meal. He was a violinist and he brought along a guitar player; the two musicians played and sang pieces from their big repertoire of folk, blues and jazz.

All of a sudden a gaunt old man with a very pronounced aquiline nose, a receding chin and shoulder-length straggly hair was standing among the guests. He must have entered the restaurant by the back door, attracted by the music that could be heard in the street. The restaurant owner told him it was a private party, but he just stood there until they brought him a glass of wine, which he paid for. One of the guests struck up a conversation with him, and he stayed a little longer and finally sat down next to the woman whose birthday they celebrated. She repeated in a rather friendly voice what the restaurant owner had already told him and then deliberately turned her back on him. In the meantime the two musicians played "Bella Ciao" and "Bei mir bist du scheen," and suddenly the gaunt man stood up and left the restaurant.

The woman breathed a sigh of relief. The disruption seemed to be over. She turned pale when a little later the aquiline-nosed, receding-chinned, straggly-haired man re-appeared at the restaurant and, stumbling playfully, nearly dropped the contrabass he was carrying.

The two musicians, both of them easy-going men, didn't know how to react, as nobody had asked the intruder to bring his instrument, and they both hated nothing more than amateurish music.

The woman seized the hand of a friend for a moment and looked at the tablecloth in front of her, tears welling up in her eyes. The violinist and the singer first looked grim, trying not to take notice of the newcomer. The man noncha-lantly took his position behind them, tightened his bow and waited until the musicians started the next piece.

To their amazement and to the disbelief of all the party guests, he joined in so easily and naturally, as if he had always been the third man. But many faces now turned first to the woman who celebrated her birthday as they all felt that the musician must bring back painful memories of her late husband.

When they noticed how she gradually relaxed, listening to the talented contrabass player and how she enjoyed the new sound and even said it was the bass that made the music complete, the spell was broken, and they started to grow enthusiastic about the surprising guest.

The bass player pulled his bow over the strings, plucked at them with his fingers or beat small rhythms on the bass with his hands, and then everybody realized how much this music needed a contrabass.

It remained a mystery how the intruder had found his way here. He only gave evasive answers and nobody knew him, neither the guests nor the people who ran the restaurant. The violinist, who had been in the music scene for thirty years, could not understand why he had never come across him before since he was an extraordinary musician, and, as he said he was 75 years old.

For a long time when the guests later remembered this party, they spoke of nothing but this contrabass player. Nobody ever saw him again. The woman wondered what had led him to the little restaurant in the suburbs on that Sunday morning. The only explanation she could think of was that her late husband had wanted her to remember him by sending her and the party guests the missing contrabass player. ooo

The End of the World

The end of the world
ladies and gentlemen
given what we know today
will go something like this:

In the beginning on a rather small island
in the South Pacific
a beetle will vanish
an unpleasant creature and
everybody will say
thank God that beetle's finally gone
it made us itch so much
and it was always so dirty.

A little bit later the inhabitants of that island will notice
that in the early morning
when the birds sing
one voice is missing
a high, rather shrill voice
like a cricket chirping
the voice of the bird whose food was, of course,
the dirty little beetle.

A little bit later the fishermen on that island will notice
that one species is missing
from their nets
the small yet especially tender fish, the one—
here I must stop for a moment and add
that the bird with the rather shrill voice
is known, or will have been known,
to swoosh out over the sea in a long loop
and on such flights it voided its droppings
and for the small yet especially tender species of fish these droppings were
its daily bread.

A little bit later the inhabitants of the continent
the rather small island in the Pacific lies near
will notice that everywhere
on the trees, on the grasses, on their doorknobs
on their food, on their clothes, on their skin and in their hair
tiny black insects are gathering
that they have never seen
and they won't understand what's going on
for they can't know, can they,
that the small yet especially tender species of fish
was food for a larger, not at all tender fish
which had simply started hunting a different species
a little yellow stickleback of the same size

that mostly fed on those black insects.
A little bit later the inhabitants of Europe
that is, you and I
will notice that egg prices are rising
and quite a bit indeed
and the chicken farmers will say
that the corn
which most of the chicken feed is made of
can suddenly no longer be had
from the continent the rather small island
in the Pacific lies near
because of some kind of plague of insects
which was successfully headed off with poison
but that unfortunately wiped out the corn, too.

A little bit later
now it gets faster and faster
nobody will eat any more chickens.
In the search to replace the corn in the chicken feed
the amount of fish meal was doubled
but it's just that every fish today has
its own particular mercury content
it used to be low enough that nobody was contaminated
but now the chickens are dying all over the world.

A little bit later
the inhabitants of that rather small island
in the South Pacific

will run in horror from the shore into the houses
after seeing something never seen before.
On that day the high tide
and it must also be added that
the sky was blue and there was no wind
and the waves were low, as they always were
when the weather was fine
and still on that afternoon
the shore of the island was under water
and of course nobody knew
that on that same day all over the world
the people ran from the shores into the houses
and saw the rising of the sea for what it was.

A little bit later
the inhabitants of that rather small island
in the South Pacific
will climb from the roofs of their houses
into the fishing boats
to sail toward that continent
where earlier the thing with the corn had happened.
But there too the sea has already risen and risen
and the coastal cities and the harbours, they are
already deep under water
for the thing of it is
that all of the fowl
six billion birds
given how poisoned they were

had had to be burned
and the soot from the fires
was the proverbial straw
for an atmosphere
already on the edge from heat and burning.
It let the sunlight in as it always had
BUT IT DIDN'T LET IT OUT ANYMORE
which warmed the air so much
the ice at the poles began to melt
the cold was no longer cold
and the seas rose.

A little bit later the people
who fled to the mountains in the meantime
will spot an odd, pale light
beyond the summits
far off on the horizon
and not know what to think
for it's accompanied by a slight rumbling
and if one of the older people now suspects
that this is the beginning of the battle
between the great powers
for the last remaining space for their people
then someone else will ask bitterly
how in God's name it came to this.

Well, ladies and gentlemen
the sea rose because the air grew warmer

the air grew warmer because the chickens were burned
the chickens were burned
because they were full of mercury
they were full of mercury because they were fed fish
they were fed fish because the corn no longer grew
the corn no longer grew because poison was used
the poison was needed because there were so many insects
there were so many insects
because a fish no longer ate them
the fish didn't eat them because it was eaten
it was eaten because another fish died out
the other fish died out because a bird no longer flew
the bird no longer flew because a beetle disappeared
that dirty beetle back at the beginning.

There's still another question
don't be too shy to ask it
so why'd the beetle disappear?

That, ladies and gentlemen
hasn't yet been completely explained
but I'm inclined to believe that it didn't eat right.
Instead of eating grass, it ate grass with oil
instead of eating leaves, it ate leaves with soot
instead of drinking water, it drank water with sulfur
and in the long run such behavior just comes
back to haunt you.
But there's still one more question

I'm ready to answer it
when will this happen?

That makes most of the scientists scratch their heads
they say in ten, in twenty years
perhaps in fifty or even only in a hundred
but as for me, I have my own way of looking at it
the end of the world, ladies and gentlemen
has
already
begun. ooo

Note: Franz Hohler drums a rhythm with his fingers on a table when performing 'The End of the World'. The first of many times he performed this poem was in 1973.

Coupons

It all began when I grew tired of constantly having to find new ways to say no to the cashier's question "Do you have a Supercard?" So I capitulated and send in the application form. Owning one of these cards meant that the supermarket opened an account for me that steadily accumulated points with my purchases until I had enough to order one of the items from their catalogue; a bottle cooler, a set of dumbbells, or a table grill for example. There was another advantage to owning the card; I was included in special discount promotions.

There it was lying in my letterbox, un-ordered and un-awaited, an envelope addressed to the lucky Supercard holder from which the special offers fluttered forth, coupon upon coupon! 5 cents a litre off petrol, 5 Francs off fresh fruit and vegetables, 5 Francs for the early purchase of a large quantity of Easter bunnies, 10 times the Superpoints on any purchase or 15 Francs off a purchase over CHF 100 and so on.

Obviously meticulous planning is required if I am to take full advantage of my stack of coupons, especially as they not all valid at the same time. As a non-driver I quickly got rid of the petrol coupon but after that I found myself drawing up a plan of what to redeem when so as to profit from as many offers as possible. Besides, from the very beginning I was determined not to purchase anything unnecessary that would cancel out the savings made.

And so I stood with my trolley and shopping list, to which I had attached my coupon, in the 'Super Center'; a shopping centre built with the future in mind near our house in a part of town still being developed. The upshot was, as long as the surrounding area remained unfinished, the oversized shopping centre was agreeably empty and you don't have to queue at the cashiers. It looked like the shelves were constantly being refilled which led me to wonder who needs and buys all this stuff.

So now I was one of the few shoppers and, prompted by my 10% off all 'non-food' coupon, had written a list of items which were needed in our household, for example, some tall glasses, which I discovered had been given the very original name long-drink-glasses, Champagne glasses, because they were always breaking – especially when one clinked glasses with excessive vigour – non-splatter lids for the frying pan, of which I was supposed to bring two as my wife had reminded me, a request I was happy to fulfil in light of the expected 10% discount. Candles, cleaning products, CFC-free sponges, toothpaste, organic cotton wool, recycled toilet paper, triple-action razor blades – I put them all, one by one on the conveyor belt and triumphantly presented the cashier my 10% coupon straight away – together with my Supercard. She scanned one 'non-food' item after the other, also scanning a lonely tub of single cream and a tiny brown bread roll, then she called to another cashier for help, informing me that she was new and hadn't come across this voucher before.

The other cashier took a quick look at my voucher and dryly informed me that it was only valid in the City branch. "You see?" she said and pointed to the word 'City'.

My face betrayed my disappointment. Of course she was right and I, a mere beginner in the tough sport of redeeming coupons, was wrong.

"Blast!" I said jokingly, and to my surprised I felt a genuine sense of disappointment bordering on sickening. Apparently I had been looking forward to saving 10%. Flabbergaster, I packed all the items, food and non-food, into the big rucksack in my trolley and paid the 90.50 that was due and only then did I have the idea that should have immediately come to me had I not been so stunned by this low-blow"If I buy a few more items and bring the total to over a hundred francs, would I be able to use *this* coupon instead?" I asked, and pulled from my lucky bundle the coupon promising 15 Francs off a purchase over 100 francs.

The new girl looked around for her colleague who had been able to help before and saw her standing at the next till with another cashier changing the receipt roll. She energetically shook her head no, there was no way that could be done because the transaction had already been completed.

As I let out another "Blast" a different woman, obviously some kind of supervisor, decided to get involved. She came across to our till, gave the new girl and me a motherly look and then said that it should be alright but the cashier would have to write an FM and I would have to unpack everything and put it back on the conveyor belt together with whatever I chose to buy in addition.

I agreed, squeezed passed the woman behind me to my trolley, and made for the nearest shelves where some biodegradable underwear had caught my eye. I calculated 90.50 plus the 9.90 and worked out that I would break though the sonic wall of the discount. Unfortunately, these underpants weren't available in either blue or black in my size, only a very peculiar shade of green, but I was in no mood to worry about such details. As the customer behind me, a Japanese lady gave two sales clerks the runaround, and the new girl wrote her very first FM, I began again, pulling the items from my rucksack and placing them behind the underwear on the conveyor. The cashier scanned them a second time and the display glowed with the total of 100.40. As a consumer I had run the race and won by a hair's breadth.

As the new girl took out a pen and paper and began to calculate what I still owed, I caught the unerring eye of her superior.

"Did you have one or two bottles of wine?" she asked.

I had two small bottles of white wine for cooking. "Two," I replied suspiciously.

"There's a deposit on those bottles, 30 cents each, that doesn't count as a proper purchase so that's only 99.80."

"Isn't that enough?" I asked, knowing full well that my question was entirely superfluous. Of course it wasn't enough! One hundred francs are one hundred francs. There was no way back, I was caught deep in the discount trap. I marched defiantly past the ever-growing queue to the clothing section, grabbed a second pair of the really rather repugnant green underpants and laid them like a sacrificial offering in front of the cashier. She punched the poison-green 9.90 into her till, recalculated how much I had to pay, a rather complicated sum, 110.30 minus 90.50 equals 19.80, minus my 15 franc discount leaves a total of 4.80. So at the end of the day I paid 4.80 for two pairs of disgusting, although ecologically sound, underpants that I didn't actually want.

The new girl thanked her supervisor. She would never have been able to do that on her own she said, sending me a dubious look. I thanked both of the self-sacrificing sales girls but it took me a while to recover from the exertion of my hard-won discount and it wasn't until I got home and looked at my receipt that I realised I had profited: my 89 Supercard points from the FM hadn't been cancelled! There they were, credited to my account. I had taken a step closer to being able to order a cut glass elephant or a 'life hammer' which could smash any car window and whose blade was sharp enough to even cut through seat belts. ₒₒₒ

A Song about Cheese

Who knows the land
where everything's made of cheese
really everything of cheese?
The houses are of cheese
the streets are of cheese
the trees are of cheese
and the flowers are of cheese
the trams are of cheese
the cars are of cheese
the churches are of cheese
and the bells are of cheese
everything's of cheese, of cheese, of cheese!

And people all wear
Coats made of cheese
wear glasses of cheese
and read their books of cheese
full of words of cheese
about things of cheese
watching films of cheese
in cinemas of cheese
they buy tickets of cheese
for a city of cheese
of cheese, of cheese, of cheese.

That wouldn't be so bad
but the air is of cheese
and the water's also of cheese
the clouds are of cheese
the sun is of cheese
the moon is of cheese
and the stars are of cheese
the apples are of cheese
the pears are of cheese
the milk is of cheese
and the bread is of cheese
everything's of cheese, of cheese, of cheese.

The worst of it is
even people are of cheese
and give kisses of cheese
have a heart of cheese
and tongues of cheese
speak a language of cheese
and thoughts of cheese
say prayers of cheese
to a god of cheese
have dreams of cheese
where they dream how it'd be
in a country without cheese

but also those dreams
are of cheese. ooo

The Dying Man

During the short time I ring the doorbell, enter, greet his wife and take my coat off, to her dismay he has got out of bed, now stands by the window and wants to open it. She asks him to go back to bed. It doesn't take much to persuade him and I help her to lay him down. He has become very light, this 88-year old man. And as he is lying there again, as is expected of a dying person, and has even folded his cold hands on the sheet, he explains to me why he got up.

"It is necessary," he says, "to shout out of the window: 'Vivent les boules rouges — toutes allumées!'" *

I ask him if he wants me to do this for him, and he nods. So I open the window and shout into the garden: "Vivent les boules rouges — toutes allumées!" Outside there is a lot of coming and going, a fact that his wife and I haven't noticed before.

"On the canal," says the dying man, "strong youths are going to and fro in their boats. There are punts which they move with the help of long poles. Among them there are three strong men. One of them is the Schnetzel-mann."

---

*"Vivent les boules rouges — toutes allumées!" means 'Long live the red balls — all lit'

I have brought a big bunch of summer flowers. After his wife and I have chosen a vase, I take the flowers into his room and set them down where he can see them from his bed.

He has us raise the head of his bed and says, "Now check if there are any more of these bunches of flowers."

"This is the only one," says his wife, and asks, "Do you know the name of the big yellow flowers that are part of the bunch?"

He ponders for a long time to find a name for the sunflowers and finally decides on "horse flowers."

"Tomorrow," he says, "I want to put on my clothes again."

"Tomorrow is Sunday," replies his wife. "Tomorrow we are not doing anything."

"Oh, Sunday," he says and proclaims "I want to go to the St. Ursen church!" We should get his clothes ready, and his son could pick him up. "Solothurn is a town with lots of water," he adds, and asks, "can you see water from the window?"

"Solothurn," I answer, "has a wonderful river, the Aare, but I can't see the Lake of Zurich from your window, it is somewhat beyond my view." There is so much water all around him, but he is drying out. He doesn't drink enough and not even through the infusion tube does his old body get enough liquid.

Suddenly the dying man asks me, "Is it a special Sunday tomorrow?"

I think for a moment and reply, "Tomorrow we are going to vote."

"Ah, a voting Sunday." He breathes a sigh of relief and says, "In that case I hope we'll get a good new constitution."

"I hope so, too," I say. "And in any case I'll vote for the new constitution."

"The voting might start tonight at ten o'clock," he says, dismissing us to make himself more comfortable.

I can't imagine what he means when he talks about the stucco work he sees on the ceiling. Looking at the stripes in the wallpaper, he calls them vocal cords and asks if I have brought them with me.

"No," I say, "They were here before." As I give him my hand to say goodbye, I thank him for his daughter, who is my wife.

"In that case, you have to thank my father, too," he says smiling, "because without him I myself wouldn't be here." Suddenly his eyes are shining with tears and he thanks me for marrying his daughter, as the two of us make a nice couple.

I wish him a good rest and make for the door, and later when I leave the house, I am very careful not to fall into the canal where strong ferrymen take their passengers across to the big party in honour of the new constitution, for which all the red lamps are already lit. ∞

In Another Country

As the Greek grocer is weighing Sicilian artichoke hearts for me, a young man enters the shop and asks "Here shop portugues?"

"No," the grocer replies, "there's only an Italian shop on the other side of the railway station and a Spanish one in Seebach, another part of town."

"Shop portugues?" asks the other man again. Apparently he hasn't been understood.

But the Greek has understood him perfectly. "No," he says. No, that's all there is here.

The man from Portugal still cannot believe it and asks the question for the last time, but this time without a question mark: "No shop portugues."

That's right. No shop portugues, not here where he works, and for a moment he keeps looking at the dried fish on display. They are, this much is clear, definitely not Portuguese fish, and he leaves the shop looking quite at a loss.

"At first when you live in another country," said the Greek, who became naturalized a long time ago, "you need such a shop to survive." The customer next to me with the Hungarian bell pepper in his hand adds: "What you eat the first twenty years of your life, you eat for the rest of your life."

He speaks almost without an accent. ₒₒₒ

Visiting Ancestors

Recently my father and I spent an afternoon together with our ancestors. They are found in the registry office of my official home community. Records go back to 1648 when a clergyman started a registry of births, marriages and deaths in neat handwriting after the old registry had not survived the Thirty Years' War. The clerk at the community office carefully stacked the books in front of us, handling them as if he were carrying a living being in his arms.

If you want to find out something about your ancestors, you start with someone whose name you know – for example, with your great-grandfather. Look in the registry under his date of birth, find registered there who his parents were, search their date of birth, maybe find it, maybe there are several people of the same name, don't try to trace your mother's ancestors for the moment since the male ancestors are considered more important, and in the end you come to a name you can almost be sure goes as far back as you can go.

My oldest recorded ancestor was Hans Friedli Hohler. He was already married when the registry was started. He had eight children. Three of them were called Johannes. The first two died at birth, but the third was viable. Later though, I read under 'nomina defunctorum' that he died when he was 18 years old. When searching for your ancestors, it is pleasing to think you are somehow connected to these people without knowing the slightest thing about them. Maybe there is still a trait you have from them, a gesture or a way of behaving that would make someone who lived at the time of Hans Friedli say about you: just like Hans Friedli.

My family name is rarely heard today, so rarely that when I meet someone with this name I get curious. If a 70-year-old Hohler tells me that when he was young, he and his five brothers formed a brass sextet and played dance music, somehow I feel proud as if it had something to do with me. Also when I learn about the theatre performances, men's choirs and yodelling quartets, it seems to me that exactly in this village and exactly with these people there is something in the air, a joy in useless beauty, in a fundamental form in which I recognize myself.

But when turning through the pages at the registry office, the seldom found name becomes ever less seldom. Hundreds of people show up who turned around when you called them by such a name. There were many with first names like Barnabas, Wunibald, Fridolin, Abraham, Euphrosine. Coming across the name Albertine Hohler, my father recalls that his grandmother still remembered this woman.

There have also been a lot of Franz Hohlers. One was a clerk at the community office, and I find an even earlier one who died on October 22, 1746. "De arbore lapsus," the clergyman wrote in addition, meaning 'fell from a tree', and continued that after the fall he still lived in pain another 14 days before dying. In 1904 another Franz Hohler drowned in the Limmat – the reason isn't given. And another one, a brother of my great-grandfather, emigrated to America in 1879. Relatives later showed us a letter where the death of a Frank Hohler was announced, probably the emigrant's son. In this letter written twelve years ago, it says, "Frank was blessed with a happy disposition. He could sing and laugh and joke up to the last minute."

For several moments a certain coldness is emitted from the book when at the christening of a child it is said of the parents, "vagabundi et acatholici." Or when next to two other "vagi," Anna Maria Büechlerin and Johannes Kuder, is written: "patriam habent nullam," they don't have a fatherland. The school Latin of the village clergymen is a language I understand, ad aeternitatem migravit, he wandered into eternity, repentina morte obiit, died a sudden death, or about an old man: senex ac mendicus, a very old man and even a beggar. My native place was at that time still a part of Austria. Therefore it's also unusual, sounding almost like a privilege when it says next to the place of origin: Ex Helvetia. From Switzerland.

Towards the end of an afternoon with these books, there is not much left of the slowness, tranquility and quietness of the past. It seems there is a concentration of the birthing and dying, a haste so great that one of the clergymen writing the entries did not even make an effort to list a newborn who had died shortly after birth in the list of deaths. Instead he crossed out, actually blocked out the name with two heavy dark strokes of his quill pen, finished, dead, the next one, three Johannes, four Johannes, five Johannes, until finally one survives. When a man's wife dies, he marries again and fathers another child so that in these times of sudden death as many living beings as possible can be left.

For almost a quarter of a century an Isaak Hohler was always witness to marriages. He was perhaps a good entertainer or a wealthy man, or both. Now that there is nobody around to talk about him, he is only one who during those days hurried from one wedding celebration to the next. In the registry, life gets shortened, a date for the birth, a second date for the death. For every person living today there is a little empty space lurking on paper, ready for the second date. The inevitability that sooner or later a community's registrar will enter those few digits, the day, the month, and the year, makes everything happening in between so quick and futile that thoughts of the village theatre, brass sextet and yodellers almost bring tears to one's eyes.

In the past, nights must have been darker. ooo

The Mailbox

"I wish I were a racing bike," said the mailbox to the garden gate, "and could flit through wide plains and conquer mountain passes."

"You and your wishes," croaked the garden gate, "when you don't even meet the official postal regulations."

"One can always wish," sighed the mailbox, and continued to swallow bills, magazines, advertisements and postcards.

A little later he was unscrewed and replaced with a new one. He was melted down. Then together with old metal chairs, torn wire fences and bent screwdrivers, he was processed into light steel, landed in a racing bike factory, and was soon flitting across wide plains and conquering mountain passes and could hardly believe that he had stood for years in the same place and every day nearly choked on the mail. ooo

About Franz Hohler

Franz Hohler was born on March 1, 1943, in Biel, he grew up in Olten, where he says he

". . . played games, sang and played music, pretended to be on stage, spent time pondering things, writing, dreaming, together with a brother who liked to play as much as I did and with parents who liked music and theater and who loved to read. As soon as I could read, I spent a lot of time among our many books, and the first time I came across the word 'culture' I thought I knew what that was because we had it at home. As soon as I could read, I also began to write — little stories, little poems or verses that I illustrated myself as I had seen done in the Wilhelm Busch and Globi books. I had the feeling that a story was not finished when it was written, but that it also had to be performed."

While in school in Aarau, he was moved by seeing Max Frisch's play 'Andorra'. He took some drama lessons in Zurich from the widow of Alexander Moissi, and also had cello lessons from Hans Volkmar Andreae, a student of Pablo Casals. In 1963 in Aarau he passed the Swiss examination qualifying him to study at a university. That year he began his studies of German and Romance Languages at the University of Zurich where he stayed for five semesters.

Two possibilities kept going through his head: He could become a school teacher. Or he could continue being a dreamer, a poet, singer and performer who made a living from his ideas. In 1965 he decided on the latter. He collected his poems, texts, songs, parodies and fantasies and put them together to make a musical-satirical solo program that he called "pizzicato." He asked the rector of the university for permission to use for his performance the cellar where the university once had its furnaces. Franz Hohler still marvels today that this rector really gave him his permission.

That first program was a huge success and had to be prolonged. Never again would he play as many instruments as he played in his 'pizzicato' performances: cello, bassoon, clarinette, violin and viola, all kinds of flutes, harp, banjo, drums, ocarina and another half-dozen instruments. Soon he was invited to perform in Berlin, Düsseldorf, and Munich. As a writer he enjoyed trying out various forms — short stories, poems, chansons, novellas, novels, readings on stage and writing children's books. He wrote and participated in television and radio programs for children and in satirical programs on television and radio. He considers himself to be a 'literary general practitioner'.

Franz Hohler is one of the most popular and successful writers and performers in Switzerland, Germany, Austria and Liechtenstein. His performances have taken him to

Italy, Spain, Portugal, the Czech Republic, the Slovak Republic, Tunesia, Morocco, the USA, Canada, Israel, France, Sweden, Denmark, Norway, Polen, Croatia, the Netherlands, Argentina, Brasil, Chile, Australia, Bolivia and Costa Rica, Bosnia and Herzegovina, Ireland, England, Luxemburg, Romania, Greece, Venezuela, Colombia, Ecuador, India, and Belgium.

He lives in Zurich with his wife, Ursula Nagel, a psychologist and psychotherapist. They married in 1968 and have two sons.

Franz Hohler has his own very personal way of switching between and combining satire and fairy tales. Even when he is not accompanying himself on his cello, his voice has a friendly and warmly melodious tone and rhythm that can sometimes leave you laughing, or crying, or feeling the need to do both at the same time.

If you mention Franz Hohler's name today in Switzerland, you will receive smiles and hear about someone's favourite story, sketch, song or performance. The discussion can turn into an evening of shared anecdotes and memories about his writing or performances. If he is on TV or radio, nobody zaps around to other channels. He fills theatres with laughing (or pensive) audiences and easily gets whole classrooms of young children happily creating their own fantastic stories on the spot.

But Franz Hohler is not only intelligently humourous and good for many laughs. He has a big ear and a big heart for the downtrodden and participates in so many good causes and charity events that one can only wonder how he has time for his own creative projects. In his writing and performances he dares to be outspoken about political issues, uncompromising in his sense of fairness, concerned about the state of our world and our environment. With his endearing ways and many talents, it is no wonder that he has received and will continue to receive so many significant prizes and honours.

We regret very much not being able to include in this collection his most loved and talked about story 'Es bärndütsches Gschichtli' everyone knows as 'Totemügerli'. It is a three-page story that some Swiss people can recite by heart, although it is not really in the dialect of the people of Berne and nobody is sure or agrees what happens. Franz Hohler has made adaptations of it in French and in Romansh but we were unable to convince him to try it out in English, a language he speaks very well. Those of us translating his work for this collection have too much respect for his ingenuity to even try an adaptation of his 'Totemügerli'. Only he could do it.

We hope this collection of stories will enable English speakers interested in learning about and understanding the Swiss to discover one of Switzerland's finest treasures, Franz Hohler.

Dianne Dicks

For more information go to www.franzhohler.ch

Writing and performances by Franz Hohler

Solo programmes
pizzicato (1965), Die Sparharfe (1967), Kabarett in 8 Sprachen (1969),
Doppelgriffe (1970), Die Nachtübung (1973), Schubert-Abend (1979),
Der Flug nach Milano (1985), s isch nüt passiert (1987), Ein Abend mit
Franz Hohler (1990), Drachenjagd (1994), Wie die Berge in die Schweiz
kamen (1995), Das vegetarische Krokodil (1999), Im Turm zu Babel
(2000), s Tram uf Afrika (2001)

Recordings
Celloballaden, I glaub jetzt hock i ab, Ungemütlicher 2. Teil,
Einmaliges von Franz Hohler, Es si alli so nätt, Das Projekt Eden, s
isch nüt passiert, Der Flug nach Milano, Drachenjagd, Hohler
kompakt, Der Theater-donnerer, Zytlupen, Hüsch trifft Hohler, Im
Turm zu Babel, Weni mol alt bi

Recordings for children
s Zauberschächteli, Der gross Zwärg, Tschipo, Tschipo und die Pinguine,
Tschipo i der Steizit, Das kleine Orchester, In einem Schloss in
Schottland lebte einmal ein junges Gespenst, Aller Anfang

Audio books read by Franz Hohler
Zur Mündung, Bedingungen für die Nahrungsaufnahme, Die Torte und
andere Erzählungen, 52 Wanderungen, Die Steinflut, Es klopft, Das
Ende eines ganz normalen Tages

Books
Das verlorene Gähnen (1967)
Idyllen (1970)
Fragen an andere (1973)
Der Rand von Ostermundigen (1973)
Wegwerfgeschichten (1974)
Wo? (1975)
Ein eigenartiger Tag (1979)

Dr. Parkplatz (1980), in Turkish (1997), in French (2002)
Die Rückeroberung (1982), in French (1991)
Der Nachthafen (1984)
Hin- und Hergeschichten (1986) with Jürg Schubiger
Das Kabarettbuch (1987)
Der Räuber Bum (1987)
Vierzig vorbei (1988)
Die Rückeroberung (comic, 1991)
Der Mann auf der Insel (1991)
Mani Matter (1977, 1992, 2001)
Da, wo ich wohne (1993)
Die blaue Amsel (1995)
Drachenjagen, Das neue Kabarettbuch (1996)
Das verspeiste Buch (1996)
Die Steinflut (1998), in Slovak (2000), in English (2001),
       in Nepalese (2002), in French (2003),
       in Hindi (2005), in Italian (2008)
Zur Mündung (2000)
Die Karawane am Boden des Milchkrugs (2003)
Die Torte und andere Erzählungen (2004), in Greek (2007),
       in Hindi (2008)
52 Wanderungen (2005)
Vom richtigen Gebrauch der Zeit (2006)
112 einseitige Geschichten (2007)
Es klopft (2007)
Der neue Berg (2008)

Children's books
In einem Schloss in Schottland lebte einmal ein junges
Gespenst (1979), in English (1980)
Sprachspiele (1979)
Tschipo (1978), in Dutch and in Slovenian (1981),
       in Spanish (1984), in Polish (1996),
       in Bosnian (1997)
Der Granitblock im Kino (1981), in Spanish (1981),
       in Dutch (1983)
Tschipo und die Pinguine (1985), in Spanish (1987),
       in French (2008)

Der Riese und die Erdbeerkonfitüre (1993),
    in Spanish (1997)
Der Urwaldschreibtisch (1994), in Danish (1994)
Die Spaghettifrau (1998)
Wenn ich mir etwas wünschen könnte (2000),
    in Dutch, Danish, French, Swedish and
    Spanish (2000), in Hebrew (2001), in Korean (2002),
in Basque (2007)
Der grosse Zwerg und andere Geschichten (2003),
    in French (2004)
Der Tanz im versunkenen Dorf (2005)
Aller Anfang (2006), in Spanish, Galician and
    in Lithuanian (2007), in Italian (2008)
Mayas Handtäschchen (2008)

Plays (first performances)
Bosco schweigt (Theater am Neumarkt, Zurich, 1968)
Lassen Sie meine Wörter in Ruhe! (Theaterkollektiv Studio
    am Montag, Berne, 1974)
Der Riese (Volkstheater, Nürnberg, 1976)
David und Goliath (Schpilkischte, Basel 1977)
Die dritte Kolonne (Claque, Baden, 1979)
Die Lasterhaften (Theater an der Winkelwiese,
    Zurich, 1981)
Die falsche Türe (Stadttheater, St. Gallen, 1995)
Die drei Sprachen (Mladih Theater, Sarajewo, 1997)
Zum Glück (Casinotheter, Winterthur, 2002)
Television programmes
Children's programme 'Franz + René', Swiss DRS
    (1973 - 1994)
'Denkpause' Swiss DRS, 40 appearances (1980 - 1983)
'übrigens…' Swiss DRS, 46 appearances (1989 - 1994)
Filmings and parts of programmes on SF DRS, ARD,
    ZDF, ORF, 3SAT

Radio broadcasts
'Zytlupe' on Swiss Radio DRS, satirical pogrammes
    1986, 1995, 1996, 1997, 2003 - 2008
Many broadcasts for children

Films

Dünki-Schott (1986)

Der Kongress der Pinguine (1993)

Video/DVD

Drachenjagd, filmed live from the Bierhübeli, Berne (1994)

Im Turm zu Babel, filmed live from the Kleintheater,
        Lucerne (2001)

'Franz + René' films/videos

Honours and prizes

1968 Preis der C.F. Meyer Stiftung

1973 Deutscher Kleinkunstpreis

1976 Hans-Sachs-Preis der Stadt Nürnberg

1978 Oldenburger Kinder- und Kinderbuchpreis
        (for *Tschipo*)

1987 Alemannischer Literaturpreis

1988 IBBY Honour List for *Tschipo und die Pinguine*

1988 Hans-Christian Andersen Diplom

1990 *Cornichon* der Oltner Cabarettage

1991 Gesamtwerkspreis der Schweizerischen
        Schiller-Stiftung

1994 Schweizer Jugendbuchpreis for
        Der Riese und die Erdbeerkonfitüre

1995 Premio mundial "José Marti" de literatura infantil

1997 Liederpreis des SWF

2000 Prix Enfantaisie

2000 Kunstpreis der Stadt Olten

2001 Binding-Preis für Natur- und Umweltschutz

2002 Aargauer Kulturpreis

2002 Kasseler Literaturpreis für grotesken Humor

2005 Schillerpreis der Zürcher Kantonalbank
        (for *Die Torte*)

2005 Kunstpreis der Stadt Zürich

2007 Tertianum-Preis für Menschenwürde

2008 Salzburger Ehrenstier

Credits, permissions and translators

We are grateful to the publishers mentioned below for giving permission to reproduce in translation these works from copyright material.

p. 7   At Home, 'Daheim' from *Die blaue Amsel*, Munich: Luchterhand 1995, translated by Andrew Rushton

p. 8   My Mother's Father, 'Der Vater meiner Mutter' from *Das Ende eines ganz normalen Tages*, Luchterhand 2008, translated by Dianne Dicks

p. 10   The Tragic Centipede, 'Der tragische Tausendfüssler' from *Wegwerfgeschichten*, Gümligen: Zytglogge Verlag 1974, translated by Dianne Dicks

p. 11   Alternatours, 'Alternatours' from *Ticking Along Free*, Basel: Bergli Books 2000, translated by Dianne Dicks

p. 16   Conditions for Taking Nourishment, 'Bedingungen für die Nahrungsaufnahme' from *Der Rand von Ostermundigen*, Darmstadt and Neuwied: Luchterhand 1973, translated by Dianne Dicks

p. 23   The Monkey and the Crocodile, 'Der Affe und das Krokodil' from *Der Granitblock im Kino*, Darmstadt: Luchterhand 1981, translated by Dianne Dicks

p. 24   The Pet, 'Das Haustier' from *Der Rand von Ostermundigen*, Darmstadt and Neuwied: Luchterhand 1973, translator unknown, English text first appeared in the Swiss Review of World Affairs, 1973

p. 34   The Goddess, 'Die Göttin' from *Die blaue Amsel*, Munich: Luchterhand 1995, translated by Andrew Rushton

Ein eigenartiger Tag, Darmstadt: Luchter-hand 1979, translated by Katalin Fekete

p. 95   The Wild Chase on the Oberalp, 'Die wilde Jagd am Oberalp' from *Der Mann auf der Insel*, Frankfurt: Luchterhand 1991, translated by Mary Hogan

p. 98   The Caravan, 'Die Karawane' from *Ein eigenartiger Tag*, Darmstadt: Luchterhand 1979, translated by Dianne Dicks

p. 100 The Gateau, 'Die Torte' from *Die Torte und andere Erzählungen*, Munich: Luchterhand 2004, translated by Peter Routledge

p. 115 Discount Deal, 'Profitierangebot' from *Das Ende eines ganz normalen Tages*, Munich: Luchterhand 2008, translated by Katalin Fekete

p. 117 Accidents, 'Unfälle' from *Hin- und Hergeschichten*, Zurich: Nagel & Kimche 1986, translated by Dianne Dicks

p. 119 The Execution, 'Die Hinrichtung' from *Ein eigenartiger Tag*, Darmstadt: Luchterhand 1979, translated by Andrew Rushton

p. 121 Destination Selzach, 'Selzach' from *Zur Mündung*, Munich: Luchterhand 2000, translation by Dianne Dicks

p. 123 The Motorway Mystery, 'Der Geisterfahrer' from *Die Rückeroberung*, Darmstadt: Luchterhand 1982, translated by Dianne Dicks

p. 133 The Daily Death, 'Der tägliche Tod' from *Hin- und Hergeschichten*, Zurich: Nagel & Kimche 1986, translated by Dianne Dicks

p. 135 The Contrabass Player, 'Der Bassist' from *Zur Mündung*, Munich: Luchterhand 2000, translation by Elsbeth Borer

p. 138 The End of the World, 'Die Weltuntergang ', a ballad first sung in

Franz Hohler's 'Die Nachtübung' program in 1973 at the Kleintheater Lucerne, from *Der Theaterdonnerer* CD, Gümligen: Zytglogge 1995, translation by Andrew Shields

p. 145 Coupons, 'Gutscheine' from *Das Ende eines ganz normalen Tages*, Munich: Luchterhand 2008, translated by Andrew Rushton

p. 151 A Song about Cheese, 'S Lied vom Chäs' first sung in Franz Hohler's *Doppelgriffe* program in 1970 at the Theatre Fauteuil, Basel, translation by Dianne Dicks

p. 153 The Dying Man, 'Der Sterbende' from *Zur Mündung*, Munich: Luchterhand 2000, translation by Elsbeth Borer

p. 155 In Another Country, 'In einem anderen Land' from *Die blaue Amsel*, Munich: Luchterhand 1995, translated by Dianne Dicks

p. 156 Visiting Ancestors, 'Bei den Vorfahren' from *Wo?*, Darmstadt: Luchterhand 1975, translated by Dianne Dicks

p. 160 The Mailbox, 'Der Briefkasten' from *Die Karawane am Boden des Milchkrugs*, Munich: Luchterhand 2003, translated by Mary Hogan

Acknowledgments

The publisher and the author wish to thank the various translators and editors who helped select the stories and poems for this collection. Later they evaluated the translations by careful comparson with their original texts in German. Many enjoyable hours were spent in discussing how to bring Franz Hohler's language and storytelling skills into English.

There can never be a perfect translation, but we hope this book enables people who cannot read his work in German to discover the wide range of talents this Swiss writer has and to understand why so many Swiss are prond of him.

Special thanks go to Mary Hogan, Anne-Louise Bornstein, Elsbeth Borer, Andrew Rushton, Katalin Fekete, Patricia Eckert, Viviane Kammermann, Peter Routledge, Andrew Shields, Kris Germann, Mitchell Bornstein, Scott MacRae, Beth Reigbar and Loretta Strauch.

We are also grateful to Pro Helvetia, the Swiss Arts Council, and to the Lotteriefond der Kanton Solothurn for their support of this book.

About Bergli Books

Bergli Books publishes, promotes and distributes books, mostly in English, that focus on living in Switzerland.

Ticking Along with the Swiss edited by Dianne Dicks, entertaining and informative personal experiences of many 'foreigners' living in Switzerland. ISBN 978-3-9520002-4-3.

Ticking Along Too edited by Dianne Dicks, has more personal experiences, a mix of social commentary, warm admiration and observations of the Swiss as friends, neighbours and business partners. ISBN 978-3-9520002-1-2.

Ticking Along Free edited by Dianne Dicks, with more stories about living with the Swiss, this time with also some prominent Swiss writers, including Franz Hohler, Hugo Loetscher, Gisela Widmer, Emil Zopfi, and -minu. ISBN 978-3-905252-02-6.

Cupid's Wild Arrows – intercultural romance and its consequences edited by Dianne Dicks, contains personal experiences of 55 authors living with two worlds in one partnership. ISBN 978-3-9520002-2-9.

Laughing Along with the Swiss by Paul Bilton has everything you need to know to endear you to the Swiss forever. ISBN 978-3-905252-01-9.

Once Upon an Alp by Eugene Epstein. A selection of the best stories from this well-known American/Swiss humorist. ISBN 978-3-905252-05-7.

Swiss Me by Roger Bonner, illustrations by Edi Barth. A collection of playful stories about living with the Swiss by a Swiss/American humorist. ISBN 978-3-905252-11-8.

A Taste of Switzerland by Sue Style, with over fifty recipes that show the richness of this country's diverse gastronomic cultures. ISBN 978-3-9520002-7-4.

Berne – a portrait of Switzerland's federal capital, of its people, culture and spirit, by Peter Studer (photographs), Walter Däpp, Bernhard Giger and Peter Krebs. ISBN 978-3-9520002-9-8.

Beyond Chocolate – understanding Swiss culture by Margaret Oertig-Davidson, an in-depth discussion of the cultural attitudes and values of the Swiss for newcomers and long-term residents. English edition ISBN 978-3-905252-06-4. German edition ISBN 978-3-905252-10-1.

Lifting the Mask – your guide to Basel Fasnacht by Peter Habicht, illustrations by Fredy Prack. Whether you are a first-time visitor or a life-long enthusiast, here's all you need to know (and more) to enjoy Basel's famous carnival. English edition ISBN 978-3-905252-04-0. German edition ISBN 978-3-905252-09-5.

Culture Smart Switzerland – a quick guide to customs and etiquette by Kendall Maycock provides crucial insights to business culture to help newcomers navigate their way quickly through Swiss life and society. ISBN 978-3-905252-12-5.

Hoi – your Swiss German survival guide by Sergio J. Lievano and Nicole Egger, chock-full of cartoons, tips and encouragement to help you learn Swiss German, includes English and Swiss German dictionaries. English edition ISBN 978-3-905252-13-2. German edition includes German and Swiss German dictionaries ISBN 978-3-905252-14-9. French edition also includes French and Swiss German dictionaries ISBN 978-3-905252-16-3.

Swiss Cookies – Biscuits for Christmas and All Year Round by Andrew Rushton and Katalin Fekete, with twenty-nine popular and traditional Swiss cookie recipes from Betty Bossi. ISBN 978-3-905252-17-0.

Ticking Along with Swiss Kids, by Dianne Dicks and Katalin Fekete, illustrations by Marc Locatelli. A colourful and fun way for children from ages 6 to 12 to learn all they need to feel at home and learn about Swiss languages, food, festivities, what kids read, sing, play and how they get along. Includes songs with their musical scores, a one-act play, maps, lists of places to visit and a 32-card language game, photographs and playful cartoons and illustrations throughout. ISBN 978-3-905252-15-6.

More information about Bergli Books can be found at www.bergli.ch